BLUE shift

DELIA STRANGE

Paperback ISBN: 978-0-9944614-8-3
Digital ISBN: 978-0-9925201-1-3

www.DeliaStrange.com

1231 Publishing
PO Box 77
Kallangur Q 4503
AUSTRALIA

ACKNOWLEDGEMENTS

I wish to thank the Strathpine Writers' Group for being supportive and constantly available, and for assigning homework tasks to inspire the writers that visit. If not for this group, *Second Life* would not exist. Special mention must go to Ray See for challenging me to set a story in a rural setting.

I also would like to thank the wonderful ladies who participate in the 'Critique Club' and who've given me much needed feedback on multiple stories and projects. Lorraine Slim, Fiona Latham, Christine Connor and Tammie Meijer. Getting together is too much fun.

And of course I must thank my constant, both in friendship and in writing; Linda Conlon.

ABOUT THE AUTHOR

Delia Strange has always had a love affair with books. As a child, the bookshelf couldn't be filled quickly enough and stories were read over and over. Trips to the library yielded gifts far superior to the latest expensive gadget toy as seen on TV. Once Delia became the creator of stories, nothing gave her more pleasure than writing them, until she started sharing them.

Delia Strange lives in sunny Brisbane, Australia along with her husband, young daughter, and two cats.

CONTENTS

SECOND LIFE
CHAPTER ONE

I wake up terrified. What pulls me from sleep aren't the terrors of my own mind—they are his. The scream lingers in my ears like looped audio. I throw the bedcovers off and run down the narrow corridor to Popsy's room. All I hear now are the thud of my footsteps on the floorboards and the creak of a bedroom door behind me. I know Hope must be watching my back; my spine tingles with the weight of her intelligent eyes. I ignore the sensation and enter Popsy's room.

He's sitting up. His silhouette is poorly framed in the bedroom window. There's not much light to see by as the moon is a sliver. I know why he's having a bad dream but I don't address it, I just flip the switch.

Popsy squints against the harsh glow that floods his room, but he doesn't look upset by my action. When the bad dreams come he always asks for the light and now he no longer has to. He's an old man but we all do it, we all ask for the light after our bad dreams.

He presses his palms to his eyes and my heart

aches at the sight. He looks like a terrified little boy in an old man's skin. I approach and sit on the foot of his single bed. Eventually his hands settle on his lap and I see embarrassment behind a soft smile.

"You're a good girl, Bunny. I'm sorry I woke you."

Popsy has always called me Bunny and I've always called him Popsy; as does the rest of the town. None of us know his real name. Even though I'm known as Brenda, I secretly prefer being called 'Bunny' though it doesn't suit a woman approaching forty. Popsy could be my father and Hope could be my child, and we all live together in a small country town called Dungoora. It's the perfect masquerade.

The next morning brings the smell of scrambled eggs. I'm still dressed in my sleeping outfit of a tee-shirt over boxers. Hope is seated at the breakfast table, fully clothed and her blonde hair in low pigtails. She is reading a book intended for an age more advanced than her eight years. Usually she can cope but this morning she is frowning at it. Perhaps she's chosen something too ambitious.

"Morning, Popsy," I say with a smile and am greeted enthusiastically with an order to pour some orange juice. I dutifully do so and place three glasses at their places around the breakfast table.

"Thank you, Mummy," Hope says, closing her book so she can smile at me. The look on my face takes it away and I regret whatever my expression was when she hastily flips through pages to find where she's last read. I can't tell if she's holding in tears or if she's angry.

"You're welcome, Hope," I say belatedly. It isn't enough and as I lower myself onto my chair I look pleadingly at Popsy who approaches with three plates balanced in his work-roughened hands. He shakes his head and I press my lips together, taking his advice. Too little, too late. I will have to make it up to her if I want this family to hold together.

Hope goes to the tiny school that boasts fourteen students of various ages. Popsy goes to work at the bakery, where he has discovered a wonderful skill for making breads and pastries. I go to the small single-roomed building that serves as the town's council chambers. This isn't my main job—I normally move between managing the library and teaching at the school, but the library is closed until tomorrow and it's not my turn to teach this week.

My morning is filled with negotiations and hearings. The townsfolk approach the council with their problems and we all try to solve them together. The sense of community is strong and every issue is sorted with a handshake. Nothing divides us on the eve of a new moon. We are all running on nervous energy. It's easy to understand the panicked stares on people's faces as they talk rapidly, trying to hide their apprehension. I can feel it too, thrumming inside of me like I'm a battery being overcharged.

"Brenda."

I am on the doorstep and turn to see Enzo stride towards me. I step aside so I'm not blocking the doorway and notice two of the town gossips grinning at us with interest from across the street. I try to ignore them but can't, they are in my peripheral vision. Enzo blocks them with his muscular frame and I'm both relieved and worried. I like him but I haven't made up my mind yet and gossip in this town is enough to partner two people for life.

"How's Popsy?"

Concern on his face makes me feel guilty. Enzo is a good man, I could hardly do better.

"He's alright. Did he wake you?"

Enzo lives two houses down from us and it's likely Popsy's screams were heard beyond our immediate neighbours. It was very early morning.

Enzo shakes his head. "I was awake."

Even though it's an unusual time of night to be awake, I don't question or doubt him.

"He doesn't dream often," I say.

"Neither do you," Enzo remarks.

I look at him with confusion. How could he know such a thing? He sees my expression and chuckles. His laughter is warm and light and I bask in it. Laughter is valuable here. I don't worry whether he is laughing at me or not, I simply enjoy it.

"I'm taking the truck into the city today."

I wonder why he's telling me this as Enzo takes Gabriel with him to help with the shopping.

"Did you want to join me?" he asks when I'm silent for too long.

"Won't Gabriel be coming too?"

He looks a little flustered and I wonder why. The conversation isn't a difficult one.

"He's busy."

I blink slowly, unaccustomed to Enzo's curt

replies. I put his peculiar behaviour towards the approaching new moon.

"Wouldn't you prefer someone stronger?" I ask, thinking about what it might take to load his truck. I've seen the town's biggest muscle straining to unload bags and boxes from the truck when it returns.

Enzo chuckles like he's enjoying a joke at my expense. I don't know why my question is so humorous.

"I would like your company," he admits at last, with a hopeful tone.

The connection is finally made as I realise he's pursuing some alone time with me. I'm momentarily speechless while I debate whether to feed the rumours. My hesitation dulls the shine in Enzo's eyes so I hastily reply.

"I would like that."

My acceptance renews him and he launches into a spiel about all the supplies we need to pick up and it won't take more than a few hours. He will have me back before nightfall. For the first time I wonder if Enzo has a proposal in mind for me. I can't shake the feeling, even as we begin to walk together. He tells me about the large camping goods store he wants me to see and I'm curious. I've pitched a tent a few times but I've never taken anyone with me as my expeditions are private. While he talks I make a few noises of acknowledgement so that he knows I'm listening and he seems content with that.

SECOND LIFE
CHAPTER TWO

Gears crunch on the truck as Enzo battles it into third, making me cringe. The gearbox is old, the seats are hard, the ride is bumpy but the drive is doing me good. Wind blows my hair around my face and I close my eyes. I hear a difference in the road and smell a change in the air. I open my eyes to find we are on a metal bridge over a narrow river. The landscape here is green instead of burnt red. I can see the rooftops of houses ahead, marking the outskirts of a large town. We call it the city because to us it might as well be, it's vastly different to what I'm used to. Dungoora has under a thousand people, this place has over fifty times that.

I wind up my window when we enter town and Enzo looks over inquisitively. I smile and he smiles back. Through the glass I watch people walking dogs and mowing lawns. One man has moved an armchair onto the cramped front verandah and is sitting there, watching life go by.

We make eye contact and he scowls at me as I am driven past. Maybe he can tell I'm different. Maybe he's just a grumpy old bastard.

Enzo parks in an alley and we walk to a café. Lunchtime conversation flows freely as we talk on a range of topics, jumping from different breeds of dogs to the latest books we've read to how long it would take for the planet to mend itself if the human population disappeared overnight. He thinks a couple of years. I hypothesise fifty. We then argue what 'mending itself' means and attract stares from the other diners in our enthusiasm to prove the other wrong. When their looks cause me to grow silent, Enzo pays for lunch and we leave.

The supplies we collect are a mixture of anonymous cartons and open crates. There are a surprising number of perishables. I had no idea our townsfolk liked so much fruit. The people who work at the warehouses load them into the truck for us. While I watch them lifting and carrying alongside Enzo, I realise he hasn't taken me to the camping store yet. It is getting late in the afternoon and we still face a long drive back. I wonder if he's forgotten.

He sees me looking up at the sky and knows what I am thinking.

"Camping store next," he promises. If the place is as expansive as he says, he hasn't left me much time to look through it before night-fall. I choose not to rush him and instead give him a nod. The sensation that he has more to offer me than just a camping store persists.

With the back of the truck full of supplies, we head to our final destination. The store is as huge as Enzo promised and I'm soon lost among wide aisles overflowing with items that can make my camping trips downright luxurious. I pick up a banana steamer designed for campfires and put it down again with a smile. People will buy anything, or maybe they won't, as there seem to be a lot of banana steamers left on the shelves.

"Brenda."

I hear his voice but don't see Enzo near me. I follow where I think the call came from and find him crouched beside a large tent near the door flap. It caters for four and is beyond my needs.

"Are you starting a family?" I joke. It falls flat and he stares at me. I wonder if this is the reason he's brought me along. All day I've felt there was something on his mind and I know he's getting ready to say it. Instead of answering he pulls up a folding chair from the display nearby and gestures for me to sit while he gets another one. I wait until he settles beside me. I say nothing — this is his talk, not mine.

"Every time you pack your gear and hike away I wonder if you'll come back. It would be easier to leave, to escape." He lapses into silence and I feel guilty because his words mirror thoughts I've had. I give him the reason I stay.

"But for Popsy."

"And Hope," he adds.

"Her, too."

Something in my tone causes his eyes to shift sideways and my lips press firm.

"She's just a little girl. No more than that."

It is the first time anybody has addressed my mistrust of her.

"You don't know for sure."

"Neither do you."

I look at him and his expression is regretful while facing my scorn. He makes me feel like I am being harsh but I've beaten myself up over my stance many times and my reasons have been well thought out. In spite of my own justifications to myself, Enzo has more to say.

"Don't be swayed by her mother."

Pain hits my heart and hollows my gut like he's taken a knife to me. I am cut figuratively but there's a physical sensation that accompanies it. I wonder how long he's held his tongue, thinking these thoughts.

"You never knew her mother." Even I can hear the icy edge in my voice.

"I know you," he says, sounding cross. "I know *her*. I hear her call you her mother. I see you raising her."

"I'm not—"

"You're not a forgiving woman," he interrupts me and I am silenced in my shock. He has never been so assertive. "But forgive her. Forgive yourself."

Heat travels up my neck and tension sits in my jaw. I see fists in my lap and I make myself uncurl my fingers. A weight is pressing on my chest and I look straight ahead, unseeing. He reads my body language and says nothing more, waiting me out. We have little time to get back but he waits me out anyway. Because we have to get moving, I stand and Enzo follows my lead.

He buys the four person tent and throws the box into the back of the truck. I do my best not to look at him throughout the drive. The radio does all the speaking for us.

We get back at sunset. Strong men and women rush over from scattered locations and surround us. They are here to unload the goods as quickly as possible. Normally I would help but I am eager to get away and return home. I don't know if I'm even noticed as I leave but it feels like every eye is on me.

SECOND LIFE
CHAPTER THREE

Popsy and I are playing cards by candle-light in the kitchen. Our small table has a sheet serving as a tablecloth because Hope is underneath, pretending she's in a fort. I can see her torchlight but it barely moves as she uses it to read. I am careful not to move my feet. Even though it is late, neither Popsy nor I can sleep and there is no bedtime for Hope tonight. I doubt anyone in town is sleeping. I think of Enzo sitting alone in his house, in the dark. I do my best to focus on the game but Popsy wins yet another hand.

There are two blankets folded neatly on one of the chairs beside me. Every so often I steal a glance at them. A book lands on my toes and Hope's arms wrap around one of my legs. I put my cards down and place a hand on her head, stroking her hair.

"It's happening," Popsy says unnecessarily. I hear it, a low droning hum that gets louder as it gets closer. I reach across the table and watch as Popsy's large, gnarled hands engulf mine. When the house shudders at the foundations I hear Hope whimper and she climbs onto my lap. I hold her close as she clings to me, hiding her face in the hollow of my neck.

Above the hum I hear a different noise. A light flashes past the window at speed, a high pitched whining travels along with it. It is the leader for a large group that follow and soon all we can hear are the shrieks that accompany them as they whizz past, lighting up our kitchen in flashes. They are so loud that I barely hear Hope's sobs but I can feel her body shaking as I hold her, and her tears as they fall on my skin. I want to wrap her under the blankets but they are not for her. She will have to settle for my embrace.

When I think the shrieking lights have passed there is one left to prove me wrong, at the back of the pack. I wonder the same thing as I do every time they come; are they sentient? Do they know what they are doing, where they are going? Or are they lifeless scouts?

Then comes the silent blue light, the one that washes over our rooftops like something above is searching for us. The silence would be complete if not for Hope's sniffles. She is trying to be quiet so we can listen. There are no dogs barking, no distant lowing of cows or clucking of chickens. The window reveals nothing… nothing… nothing… then blue light fills the glass. When it disappears we know it is almost over.

The last sets of lights are worst. They are what we wait the longest for. A beacon enters through our window and throws a ring of light on the kitchen cabinets. I feel both Popsy and Hope tense and my grasp on them tightens. The ring disappears and we wait a little longer. When the clock's minute hand circles halfway around, I release Popsy's hand and stand with Hope in my arms. Once she is deposited onto Popsy's lap, I go to the window.

There is nothing to see. The street is dark and the silence complete. When I hear a dog's mournful howl in the distance I know the show is over. They don't come every time, but when they do, it is always during a new moon. I see some of the porch lights turn on and reach across to add mine. Behind me Popsy asks Hope for help to plug everything back in and she agrees enthusiastically. She has already recovered.

I am thinking about stepping out onto the front porch when I first see him. Outside it is dark but the porch lights across the street reveal his silhouette. He is walking slowly and I know he is confused. I know he is distressed and traumatised. I know this because I have gone through this myself, many years ago. I hurry to the blankets and grab them in my arms, cradling them before I go outside. I am running to him and I can see others coming out of their homes and racing towards him as well but I am the first to reach him.

In my haste to cover his nudity I drop one of the blankets. I can smell him when I reach around his shoulders; he smells like a newborn infant. It is something that both comforts and horrifies me but my horror lessens when I meet his wide, terrified eyes. I feel myself transported back in time, feeling what he feels. My empathy heightens as he wraps the blanket more firmly around himself.

"You'll be okay," I tell him. My words are genuine because he is safe now and even though I don't expect an answer from him, he gives me one.

"Thank you."

More street lights blaze on, chasing away the shadows. I see that he is younger than I am. His dark hair is a curly mop atop his head but his eyes are very light. The effect is striking. He holds eye contact with me even though there are now a half dozen people around us. I touch his shoulder and he smiles at me. Nobody has behaved this way upon arrival. We were all scared and frustrated and angry.

"Where am I?" he asks. There are a few responses but because he keeps looking at me, I add mine.

"You're home."

I remember these words being said to me by a kind old man. I break eye contact with our newest arrival to see Enzo nearby. I am still hurt by his words to me earlier today though I can't properly define why. It is easier to look away. Someone has picked up the second blanket because it is no longer on the street.

I feel a strong hand grip mine and look into lovely clear eyes again.

"I don't know my name," he tells me. The welcoming committee have already begun to step away from us, giving him space because a connection is being made. It has been a long time since someone has selected me. I don't know if I can do it again but I already know this time will be different.

"You should rest now," I tell him. It will be

strange having him in my home but I have managed before and can do so again. Enzo distracts me by drawing close to us and I look at him, annoyed. I am surprised by the stern expression on his face but it softens before it is seen by anyone else but me.

"I have a spare room," Enzo says.

I want to argue this change in strategy but the silence of everyone around us tells me they wish not to interfere further. Enzo has broken protocol and I don't know what to do. My indecision causes the stranger to draw closer to me which makes up my mind.

"Enzo will look after you."

As much as I want to form a new connection, I understand the obligations that come with it will only weigh me down.

SECOND LIFE
CHAPTER FOUR

When I enter the house again it is still. I turn off the porch light and wait for my eyes to adjust to the darkness. My mind turns over what just happened and I can feel a hot lump of fury at the base of my throat. Enzo's interference has left me to weather an emotional storm. I hear the wooden floor creak under the pressure of footsteps before Popsy's soft shuffle brings him to me.

"You alright, Bunny?" he asks. He bathes me in sharp, fluorescent light and I can see he is taken aback by my expression. "What happened?"

I stride to the breakfast table and sit carelessly on one of the chairs. It protests with a wobble but doesn't spill me to the floor.

"I made a new connection," I blurt out, doing my best to contain the volume. Hope must be in bed by now.

Popsy lowers onto the chair opposite. His question to me is measured, thoughtful.

"Did you want to make one?"

His words come with the implication that I didn't.

"I wouldn't refuse it," I say. I realise this is not a yes and reconsider my decision to let my stranger go. I think of his lovely clear eyes and the smile he offered me and I don't want him to suffocate on the choke-hold of this town. It will drown him as it has drowned me.

"How was your connection lost?" he asks. His gnarled fingers twitch with the desire to hold my hand. Popsy is a man who comforts with hugs and touches. I am a woman who likes my space. We both make compensations for the other and he respects my preference. He knows I have been wronged.

"Enzo interfered."

Popsy's eyebrows rise slightly. It is a minor expression and I wonder if he knows that he's made it.

"Your connection was with a man?" Popsy guesses. He is very quick to reach the same conclusion I have; that Enzo's action was driven by jealousy. If my connection was with a woman, I doubt he would have interfered. I would also be more likely to break the connection myself, if I'd made it at all.

"I am sick of having my life planned out for me, or my decisions made for me by others," I hiss. I need to get my frustration out and it comes as a tidal wave, words pouring over one another and washing away every reasonable thought. "I'm praised for my strength or told I need to be more forgiving. I'm only allowed to connect with those others approve of. I am told I shouldn't leave and then face surprise when I come back. Everybody tiptoes around me because of *her*. My life has been decided for me because of *her*. For a single moment I chose for myself and it was taken from me. How about what *I* want? How about *I* make a choice who I live with?"

When I am done I realise what I have said. My cheeks flare pink and I press my lips firm so no more can escape. Popsy is unmoved, a statue in the face of my wrath. There is a lot more bottled up inside of me but he is the wrong person to unleash my concerns on. It is Enzo who deserves my wrath.

When I speak again, I am calm. I have had years of practise swallowing my ire.

"He changed the rules," I whisper. My words are hypocrisy in the face of what I've just said. I have railed against the rules and now I complain that they aren't being followed. I do not know what I want. I want to scream my confusion but will have to make do with my soft protest.

Unbelievingly, Popsy says: "He is trying to protect his woman."

"I am not his woman," I say firmly and in a normal speaking voice. It is the loudest declaration I can muster to not disturb the sleeping child in the house. "I am my own woman."

Popsy nods and gets up from the chair. He bids me goodnight and I say nothing in return.

After some time I realise how sharply I've spoken. I go upstairs and stand at the doorway to his room so I can apologise but he is already asleep and breathing deeply. History dictates there will be no dreams tonight and I do not wish to wake him.

I shower and dress for bed. Under the covers I press my face into the pillow to conceal my sobs until the despair passes and I am calm enough to sleep.

The security screen covers a white painted door. I stare at it for a long moment, aware at how clean both doors are. It speaks of the man who lives in this house. I bang my fist on the frame of the screen and it gives a satisfying rattle. Enzo answers it and looks at me, lost for words.

"Did you not expect me?" I ask. My tone is gentle as I am over the initial rage from last night.

"I never decided what I wanted to say," Enzo admits.

"Let me in," I tell him and he steps aside. I had anticipated an apology and am disappointed it didn't come. I move past Enzo into his house. I haven't been in here before and am surprised to see a vase filled with wildflowers on a low coffee table. They are the only feminine touch in a room dominated with woods and dark colours.

"Where is he?"

Silence meets my question and for a moment I

think he's not going to tell me.

"In the backyard."

I move through the unfamiliar house with Enzo trailing behind me and find a sliding door that has been pushed wide open. Outside I see my stranger on a lounger, sunning himself. As I approach, his eyes open and he quickly gets to his feet. I don't protest because it is sweet. For someone forming a new set of memories, he certainly recalls good manners.

"How are you doing?" I ask. He reaches a hand towards me and I instinctively take it. I feel abnormally comfortable with him and I don't know why. I am fascinated by him—he is unlike anyone I have ever met, or remember.

"Better now," he says and I shake my head at him, flattered by his words but they don't give me a genuine answer. He is properly admonished so he tips his head and tries again. "I have been picking a name."

I glance down at the lounger and now I can see a couple of baby names books beside it, on the ground. Enzo must have given them to him.

"I chose the name Brenda," I tell him.

"Everyone in this town chooses their names?" he asks.

"I told him we do," Enzo interrupts. I glance over, surprised by his voice because I had assumed he'd left us alone. He is standing nearby and now that I know he is there, I feel as though he is encroaching on our space. It is a ridiculous thought because we are both on his property. I turn back to my stranger.

"We all do," I say.

I wait for the rest of the questions that normally come. Questions about how much people remember. Questions about where we've all come from and why we stay here. Questions that I can't answer for anyone but myself. My stranger follows the usual pattern and asks me a question, but it isn't what I expect.

"Will you help me choose a name?"

I am the worst person he could've asked because I've put less thought into the selection of my name than everyone else in town, who deliberated for many days. I'd barely given it an hour and had become impatient with the task before I'd even reached the 'names beginning with C' page.

"I'd love to," I tell him. There is only one lounger so we take the books inside with us. Enzo follows. My stranger and I sit closely on the sofa in the front room, huddled over the first book opened to letter 'J'.

"Jacob?" he asks and I pull a face to show my uncertainty. He flips through some pages. "Jebediah?"

I look at him and try and picture my stranger as a 'Jebediah'. I can't do it so I shake my head.

"What word comes to mind when you look at me?" he asks me softly.

Lover, I almost say, but I lower my eyes and blush. I hear a snort and look over at Enzo in surprise. He is seated in an armchair and glaring at us.

"You keep searching for names, Enzo and I will get coffee and biscuits," I tell my stranger, who is also looking at Enzo. I am furious and embarrassed that his petulant behaviour is so obvious.

We both enter the kitchen, which has a swinging door to enclose us and our whispered conversation. Enzo fills up the kettle while I hiss at his back.

"What are you doing? Why are you snorting and scoffing and hovering?"

Enzo places the kettle on the cooktop and turns to face me.

"It's ridiculous," he says.

"What's ridiculous?" I demand, wanting him to make a statement so I can attack it.

If it lies unspoken, it can never be addressed. I want no more miscommunication between us. I have already fooled myself with the thought of his proposal—one that never came. There is no sense in prolonging this conversation.

"He's half your age," Enzo says.

"How dare you?" I seethe. "You don't know his age. You don't know *my* age."

"I still have eyes," Enzo counters.

I am insulted by his declaration that I look old. "Eyes you may have, but no heart and no sense."

"You speak to me of sense? What sense is there in pursuing a man so wrong for you?"

"What sense is there in pursuing a woman who doesn't want you?" I reply coldly.

His eyes widen and his mouth forms a circle of surprise like he has been slapped. If I had struck his face I think it would hurt less. I want to take it back but I also don't. He has to know. The surprise leaves behind sourness and he grunts a reply. "Make an excuse and leave."

I am shocked by his order to leave the house. He has politely thrown me out. I hesitate while I consider my options. There are not many; I can leave or I can make a plea to stay. While I decide, Enzo turns his back and I realise I have missed my chance to speak. I exit the kitchen.

My stranger is studying the names book intently and doesn't notice me until I tell him that I have to go to work now. He looks at my artificial smile with puzzlement. I escape the room in long strides, making sure not to slam the doors behind me because I don't want to give further clues that something is wrong. I realise how silly I'm being because it is already apparent but I can't help trying.

I struggle to hold in my emotions on the short walk back to my empty house. With Popsy at the bakery and Hope in school I have nobody to comfort me. The instant the front door is shut at my back I take in a loud, sobbing breath and cover my mouth with the back of my hand. I hate crying. I hate how it makes me feel; weak and desperate.

It takes me less than a minute to get myself under control. It is long enough for me to wipe my tears and take a calming breath, and also long enough for someone to arrive and knock on my door. I don't want to answer it because I think I know who it is, but Enzo deserves a chance to be heard. We have always done that for each other.

When I open the door I find my stranger.

"Are you alright?" His first question is gentle, compassionate. He reaches a hand out for me across the threshold and I lead him inside the house. I shut the door behind him and turn the lock. It grudgingly yields to my pressing thumb.

When I turn to face him he is very close and my heartbeat picks up. The physical response I have to him is overwhelming. I am aware the attraction I have for him is shallow, but to its credit, it is mutual.

My stranger holds both my hands in his. This is a favourite interaction of his, as this is the second time he's done this with me.

"Were you and Enzo together?" he asks me. His use of tense informs me that he has already decided we are not currently partnered.

"No." I want to say more but am unable to. Even this single word was difficult to summon. I am looking at his mouth and I lick my lips. This action wasn't planned and makes me feel brazen. I lift my gaze from his mouth and into lovely clear eyes. We are standing closely together, my breasts brush his chest. I wonder if he can feel the hardened nubs of my nipples and imagine him suckling on them. The thought is enough to make me close my eyes in attempt to cast it away, but the opposite is true. He releases my hands and wraps his arms around me, pulling me close. Our embrace is intimate. He lowers his head to breathe a statement near my ear.

"I would like us to be."

His breath is warm and washes over my face with the faint aroma of cinnamon, like he has enjoyed something sweet for breakfast.

Heat pulses between my legs at the thought of us being together. I wonder if he meant something beyond the physical but I don't care. I want him with a force that surprises me and makes me feel vibrant. The sensation is one that is both familiar and unrecognisable. My lust for him seems insatiable but I plan on putting it to the test.

I turn my head and tilt my chin to meet his already seeking lips. It appears neither of us can wait. His hands first press me close and then explore my body, groping everywhere with a need that I match. His body is firm and exciting; everywhere I touch finds muscle and I can't remove his clothing quickly enough. His shirt is only half-off revealing a well-toned torso, when his hand moves inside my underwear. One of his fingers slides easily within me. He watches my face and holds me close as I buck and thrust against him on watery legs.

The door becomes a tool to help me keep my feet as his fingers—two of them now—seek deeper before pinching and teasing the nub that causes me to bite his shoulder. He grunts the pain of my teeth on his flesh and I swap my mouth for clinging hands instead. With my jaw clenched, I hold him as he strokes me to orgasm. The sound of my body thumping against the door matches the rhythm of our combined sighs and grunts. My body is still trembling when his fingers are replaced by his erection; long and thick and pleasantly painful until I am stretched enough to have it all.

We slide down to the floor so he can push at a better angle. With my legs tightly holding his hips, he thrusts in and out while our tongues battle between our mouths. I am lost in the whirlwind of passion he creates and each time he pounds into me it is both too much and not enough. I want more. I can't take it. By the time he reaches his own peak, I have already had another and I hold him as he trembles above and inside me. There is wonderful pulsing warmth where we are joined. My stranger has become my lover.

I am thankful for the lights that come on some new moons. They have given me the most wonderful gift.

CHAPTER SIX

We use the shower and spend most of the day languishing together in my bed. His stamina is incredible and his mouth is capable of the most delicious things. The bedcovers are puddled on the floor and I am not self-conscious as he eyes my naked body over. Desire is apparent.

"Don't tell me you can go again," I tease, hoping that he can't because I am feeling sore.

"No," he says with a growing smile before it fades into thoughtfulness.

"What is it?"

"I must be a smoker."

I hadn't expected this and laugh. Everything feels light and buoyant in my heart now that we are together. He makes me forget who I am. No, it is more than that; he makes me forget who I'm supposed to be. He has no name and when I'm with him, neither do I.

"No cigarettes?" he asks, sounding like he's already expecting a negative answer.

"Not in this house," I say, thinking of some of the townsfolk who enjoy their nicotine habit. It is not one I enjoy because of the stink. "Are you craving one?"

"I wouldn't call it craving," he says. "Perhaps a habit."

I screw up my nose. He reads my reaction correctly and shrugs.

"Everyone here comes from up there?"

I am flummoxed both by the change in topic and the direct quality of the question. It can mean so many things.

"Is that what you remember?"

He smiles at me and shakes his head. Peripherally I can see his fingers dancing a melody on his thigh. He is either used to holding a cigarette or perhaps a piano player. I stare at him until he speaks again.

"How long have you been here?"

"Eleven years."

He is silent for a long moment, looking at me. I wonder what's going on in his mind. He is not so easy to read.

"Have you ever left?"

Another loaded question but this one is easier to answer.

"I go camping on my own sometimes," I tell him, and shuffle closer so I can snuggle against him. He offers his arm as my pillow and his fingers gently strum the flesh of my shoulder. We could be teenagers. Romeo and Juliet, because it worked out so well for them. "I hike for a few days before coming back."

"But you always come back?" he asks.

The quality of his questions reminds me of Enzo at the camping store and I grow tense, thinking of him. I remember how he bought the four person tent and threw it into the back of the truck. I didn't think on it too deeply at the time but now I'm beginning to see all kinds of meanings behind it.

"Sorry," my lover whispers and I frown at him.

"What for?"

"The question makes you uncomfortable."

"Others have left," I offer him. My response earns a raised brow and I expand on the comment. "Most come back."

"And they don't speak of this place?" he asks.

I move so that I can look down at him, my head propped on one hand as my other draws lines on his chest. He is a beautiful man and I am flattered that he would be drawn to me. I am not so much of a prize.

"Would you talk about our town, if you left?" I ask him. I watch him think about the answer and all that he offers me is a shrug. "This is your home now. You can always come back here and be with people who understand. We might not know who we are or who you are, but we understand. There's a stronger connection than you might think, to that."

"I know who you are," he says to me lecherously. I refuse to be drawn into a playful mood because this is a serious topic. It is normally too early to talk of such things when someone is so new, but I've always believed that if someone is ready to ask the question then they are ready to hear the answer.

"You would turn me in?" I ask softly. He looks at me without comprehension. "You would open me up to ridicule?"

"Brenda," he says. It is the first time he has used the name I have given myself and I look at the space between us. It represents the chasm of our knowledge quite well—he both knows everything he needs to know for us to be perfect for one another and yet he has no concept of what we truly are to each other and to the world beyond. Why had I thought him so different? "You are my beacon," he says to me. My gaze lifts to meet his. "I will always be drawn to you." The words sound like something out of a movie; an historical romance perhaps.

"Always is a long time," I breathe, wishing I wasn't moved by a flawlessly delivered cliché.

"Always is a single moment in time that lasts forever," he argues, though I'm not sure it is an argument at all. If not for the brief shake of his head I would think he was agreeing with me.

"You just need something to replace your cigarettes," I point out.

He stares at me for so long that I begin to analyse the quality of my statement. Was it cruel? I meet his gaze and we are silent and watchful until I am aware that time has passed and I am incredibly hungry. Perhaps it is lunchtime. Perhaps it is beyond lunchtime. If this is the case, Popsy might be on his way home.

Without speaking I leave the bed and enter the shower again. It is still glistening and the towels have not had time to dry. I enter the spray and wonder if I have ruined something magical already. It isn't long before my lover joins me and proves that his lust for me hasn't waned. His touch is considerate and giving. He is treating me as though I am fragile.

Perhaps he has sensed something genuine from me after all.

SECOND LIFE
CHAPTER SEVEN

Popsy is the first to greet us as we sit together at the kitchen table, our lunch plates carelessly stacked to one side. My lover stands and shakes Popsy's hand and they speak freely about the bakery. Popsy is doing most of the talking prompted by my lover's questions. Once the conversation dwindles I am told that Hope plans to do her homework at a friend's house — Janina's — and will return before nightfall. I am often given news second-hand through Popsy when he delivers Hope her lunch. Popsy leaves us so he can watch his favourite show on television. He behaves as though everything is normal but I'm sure he's observed our wet hair and understands what it means.

I surprise myself by not minding his knowing.

I take my lover's hand and lead him outside. As we walk towards the small string of shops that crowd the main thoroughfare through town, I tell him about the people that live here and the children who have been born here. They are destined to leave us but would never betray their parents and extended family. They huddle in darkness on a monthly basis alongside the rest of us.

"Was Hope born here?"

The question invites my sorrow.

"Yes."

My hand is squeezed but the pain doesn't leave my heart.

"Is her father dead?"

At first I do not understand what he is asking and I look at my lover in puzzlement. His gaze is compassionate as though he understands my loss but the question is all wrong. I gradually realise he must think I'm a widow. His guess is clever but reveals how much he doesn't know.

"Her mother is dead," I say, correcting him. I watch him process this information and think about how perceptive he is, to make such a guess from small cues and vague references. I wonder if he'll make the second, deeper connection. I doubt he will because he doesn't understand the history I have with Hope. He hasn't seen us together.

"She's around ten?" he asks.

"Eight."

"You raised her," he says. I nod. "Are you worried she won't accept me?"

It is apparent to me that my lover is fond of loaded questions. I consider what part of the question to tackle when I spy some of the townsfolk staring at us. At first I think it is because my lover is new and they're curious but then I realise we're holding hands like a couple. My hand twitches with the need to pull it from my lover's hold but he tugs me closer and slows the pace so he can look at me. I relax under his gaze and release a puff of self-conscious laughter before we continue as we were. I should not be ashamed of him, or myself.

"Hope loves everyone," I say. "And everyone loves her."

"She's social?"

"And clever."

Our conversation gradually becomes one filled with introductions as we are passed in the street and the townsfolk want to meet him. It isn't difficult to introduce a man without a name because of all the practise we've had, though I struggle when the conversation turns to living arrangements and I am forced to mention he lives with Enzo. My lover gives me a long look and I wonder what he was expecting. We have been intimate and we have a connection, but I am still caught in a place between my heart and my head.

After they leave and we continue, my lover returns to his questions.

"Do I still live with Enzo?"

"It's the way things are done here."

"What things?"

I hesitate, thinking about our traditions and what they have become to us. There is a comfort to a routine that has worked for many years. It makes little sense to question it now… except the routine has already been broken.

My delay allows for another interruption and I watch as a dusty, unfamiliar red sedan slows and the window whirrs down. The passenger is a weighty, middle aged woman who gives us a hopeful smile.

"Excuse me," she calls out, even though we are both already staring at her. "Could you point us towards the hotel? The GPS can't find one for us." She makes her statement with a little shake of the head, as though the electronic device has let her down when its accuracy is flawless.

"There isn't one here, you should continue to the next town."

She looks at me like she doesn't understand what I'm saying. I can hear a shriek in the back of the car and see two children around Hope's age flinging things at one another until their father barks an order at them to stop. It has no effect.

"Is there a petrol station?" she asks finally.

"Keep going down this road past the last house, then it'll be on your right."

The window whirrs up without her thanks and the car drives away.

"Is there really no hotel in town?"

"It's boarded up," I say. Opening it up for business has been continuously discouraged.

"I bet the service station is open all hours," my lover says. "Give the tourists a full tank and send them on their way."

"We don't get many tourists, we're not on the map."

"Convenient."

I think about the red sedan arriving in the middle of a difficult question.

"Very much so."

"What about the empty houses?"

"There aren't many," I say.

"Do they get boarded up too?"

"No, they're maintained by the neighbours on each side."

"What about that one?"

I look at the house my lover is gesturing at and press my lips together. I don't like talking about other people's business and this house is certainly none of mine.

"It's lived in," I say.

"Can we visit?" My lover is crossing the road before I have a chance to answer and I can tell that I would have to make a grand declaration in order to make him stop. I shouldn't be surprised that my lover is drawn to this particular house; there must be some kind of clue that reveals its difference to the rest... though I couldn't say what it is.

As I follow him up the front path to the door, I worry about his attraction to such things and what that might say about me. He looks over at me and must see something in my expression.

"Is this place a town secret or *your* secret?"

"Town," I state. "So it's yours, too."

He smiles and takes my hand to pull me along the front walk. We both climb the three stairs that take us onto the porch. Before he knocks on the door, he looks at me inquisitively. I am composed; I don't wish to taint his discovery with my reaction.

When his knock goes unanswered, I gesture for him to enter.

"Really? Is it not rude?"

"Not at this house," I say.

The interior is gloomy because of sheer yet dark curtains. Dust mites dance on the strip of sunlight that enters with us and my lover keeps the door open wide for me to enter. After a brief internal debate, I close the door behind me. The clack of the latch as it drops back into place feels too loud. The house is quiet but not empty; even I can sense this.

"Hello?" my lover calls as he moves down the wide corridor, peering into rooms. I know the layout of this place, I used to visit often but gradually I stopped coming. I follow my lover past the sitting room and study. At the end of the corridor is the combined dining and kitchen, which is where I expect to find the occupant.

My lover disappears down a connecting corridor but I know he'll return shortly. There is nothing down there beyond a bathroom and laundry. He's back by the time I reach the junction and we both enter the kitchen together.

It is as I expected; he stands at the kitchen counter, looking out the single window not covered by a curtain. He is a tall man with silvery hair and is dressed in a grey robe over striped pyjamas.

He doesn't acknowledge us even though my lover greets him. In the silence that remains, I stare at a man who was once friendly, clever and vibrant. Now he needs someone to come by and make him food or else he won't eat, or direct him to the bath or else he won't wash, or talk to him or else he won't hear anything beyond the voices in his head. From my time spent looking after him, I know he can find the toilet by himself, and eats already prepared food. He even finds his bed on occasion.

"Doc? We have someone new in town," I say gently. Guilt threatens to swallow me because of my neglect. I couldn't bear to help him when he failed to help me. The old resentment is gone. The old hatred is gone. My head knew he wasn't to blame but my heart was filled with suspicion and paranoia. Time has apparently helped. "He doesn't have a name yet, you know how it is."

My lover looks at me as I turn to him with too bright a smile. "This is Doc Silverbeet. It's a funny name, isn't it?"

My lover frowns at me, knowing there is something amiss.

"Hello," my lover greets again, and approaches the Doc. I take a few steps backward, stopping when I bump against the doorway. My lover places a hand on Doc's upper arm and speaks softly to him. I listen to a one-sided conversation filled with observations about the town and how friendly and welcoming it is and wonder if my lover is having a bad joke at my expense. I realise he is serious as he talks about being invited to live with Enzo and making friends with me.

The mention of my name sparks movement in the Doc and I flinch in surprise. He turns and grabs my lover's arms but is looking over his shoulder towards me.

"I'm sorry about Sam," he says. "Sam wanted to be dead. No hope for that one."

His gaze drifts away when my lover asks questions. On weakened legs I make my way back through the house and throw open the door. My stomach is churning and I manage to reach the garden before I fall to my knees and start heaving on the shrubbery. Other than a few burps, nothing comes out and I manage to get myself under control.

I find my feet again when my lover joins me.

"What happened? Are you alright?"

"I'm fine," I say, my voice trembling. I wipe my mouth with the back of my hand.

"Who is he? What's wrong with him?" my lover asks. Then he tags on the question I've been dreading. "Who's Sam?"

Sam wanted to be dead.

I shake my head. I am unable to tackle his questions until I can get away from here.

We have walked around most of the town by this time, and I lead us to a small courtyard that isn't often used at this time of day. The restaurant it backs onto only operates three nights a week. My favourite night is Monday, because that's when Gayle cooks and I adore her curries.

"Doc Silverbeet was the town's doctor. I don't know why he called himself Silverbeet, but his name had everyone smiling and joking, him most of all. I think that's why he chose it."

"What happened to him?"

"He ran after the lights."

As he thinks about my statement, I reflect that he hasn't seen the lights yet since he was the last to arrive with them. I'd spoken about them while we lay in bed and he'd told me they sounded beautiful. Perhaps he might not think of them as beautiful now, after meeting Doc.

"How long ago?"

"About four years. No, wait..." I am surprised

to recall that Hope wasn't even walking yet when the Doc ventured outside for answers. Time is blending and stretching. "More like seven."

"The lights made him like that?"

"Yes."

"Has nobody else run after the lights? He was the first and only one?"

"There's only gossip. Doc is proof enough not to do it."

"Nobody's taken footage of the lights?" he asks.

I look at him, not liking the direction this line of questioning is headed. I am attracted to his differences; that his thought processes and reactions are not like anyone else in town… but that also makes him dangerous if he's not content to let things be.

"Nothing like that works when they come."

"You switch everything off," he says, nodding as though he finally understands. "Who's Sam?"

It takes me a moment to adjust. I look at my lover who is watching me closely. I dislike the sensation that he has used some kind of interrogation tactic on me in order to see my true reaction.

"A friend."

"A past lover?"

"Jealous?" I ask, smiling at him in a way that doesn't feel attractive. I drop it, imagining the kind of garish expression he's received.

"Curious," he says, placing a hand on my knee. It feels dishonest and I shift my leg. He withdraws.

"When Sam arrived in town, she and I

connected and she came to live with me." I notice my lover's eyebrows rise at my use of Sam's pronoun. "We were inseparable. Her death hit me hardest and for a long time I blamed Doc. He'd made promises to me but she ended up dying in childbirth."

I just found out he did it on purpose, I think but cannot say.

"Oh no," my lover says and immediately wraps an arm around me to hold me tight. I am smitten that he has made the connection himself, but he explains differently. "No wonder you were made sick by his words. If there wasn't something wrong with him, I'd make him apologise. Damn it, why throw Hope in your face like that?"

Hope?

I tense as I realise what he means.

No hope for that one.

I'd interpreted Doc's words as Sam's death being thrown in my face while my lover thought it was about her daughter.

My thoughts tumble over one another and throw various arguments into the forefront of my mind. While this happens I cannot do anything but sit and be held.

I am seated at the kitchen table between Popsy and my lover when Hope enters. She looks preoccupied and I wonder if things are well between her and her friend Janina. When she spies us she hesitates in the doorway. I see her eyes widen before she turns to shut the door behind her. When she looks back at us she is composed and I offer her an encouraging smile.

"Hope, you haven't met the newest member of town yet," I say. I wonder if it sounds as rehearsed to her ears as it does to mine. Hope says nothing so I fill the silence that grows pregnant with tension. "Would you like to say hello?"

"Hi," she says. The word is emotionless and dutiful. It is unlike Hope to be unfriendly and I am flustered.

Popsy asks if she has eaten dinner yet and Hope shakes her head. Popsy tells her he's made chicken hotpot and mash for dinner and I see the tension drop out of Hope's shoulders when they talk about dinner. She stiffens again when she looks at me and my lover sitting quietly together at the table and mumbles something about putting her schoolbag in her room before making a hasty exit.

When she returns she sits opposite my lover and deflects every attempt at conversation he tries to make with her. I am both embarrassed and confused by her behaviour; I've spoken highly of her and now she is showing me up. I don't know why she is so antagonistic towards my lover. The dinner conversation turns to who our neighbours are and Popsy lists off some names. As soon as he mentions Enzo, Hope interjects.

"Are you living here now, because you're not supposed to. Why don't you go home?"

"Hope!" I cry out, horrified.

"It's okay," my lover says. He gives me a soft smile and a shrug to show he's not offended, but I am offended for both of us.

"No it's not okay," I say. Hope glares and pushes away from the dinner table before standing and storming into the living room in spite of me calling her name twice. I look at Popsy but he is frowning at his plate, a fist on his chest.

"Let me talk to her," my lover says and I want to argue that he can't help because he's the cause of her hostility, but I hold my tongue. My relationship with Hope has been strained long before my lover came along. I nod and he follows after her.

I quietly eat my dinner and pour some more water in Popsy's glass who nods his thanks. I am trying to hear the conversation in the next room but it is too low a murmur for me to identify words.

My curiosity urges me to open the door between the kitchen and the sitting room. My lover and Hope are sitting on the rug beside the coffee table. Hope has her back to me and I can see my lover's face as he listens intently to what she is telling him. He doesn't glance at me and I retreat, not wanting to spoil their moment. He is getting her to talk and perhaps she needs to. I am caught in a place between dismay and pride.

After five more minutes they return. Hope apologises to us and sits down for dinner. The conversation revolves around safe topics like favourite foods and what Hope has done at school today. When our meals are finished, she clears the table and my lover washes dishes while I dry and put away. Popsy retires to bed — it's early for him but he reads. Hope goes to her room to do her homework, leaving me and my lover to sit out on the verandah and listen to the night sounds.

"I think you should go back to Enzo's now," I say, mirroring Hope's suggestion but my words are spoken regretfully.

"Hope will be okay. She's a clever girl, like you said."

"Not because of Hope," I tell him. My lover takes my hand and is quiet for a moment as he considers my words.

"Am I a fling?"

"I don't know. I didn't want you to be."

"Being with me is too difficult?"

I struggle with my answer. Being with him is easy but the circumstances are difficult. I end up not having to tackle that question because he interrupts my thinking silence with another.

"Do you want your life to change?"

I think about the constant undercurrent of sadness I feel and the desire to remain private in a town that specialises in secrets.

"I wouldn't mind if it did."

My lover puts an arm around my shoulders and holds me closer to him. I suspect he considers my answer to be one in his favour and is wise enough not to challenge me further.

The corridor looms ahead; green paint is in varying stage of peeling off the walls, revealing yellowed undercoat. It is a shade of green that makes me think of hospitals. The association fills me with dread. I move further down the corridor even though I don't want to. I look at doors to my left and right only to see each one slam shut, offering me a glimpse of clinical devices and empty beds.

I reach the room at the end of the hallway and meet resistance when I step into it. I feel like I'm walking underwater and it is this sensation that helps me to realise I am dreaming.

The knowledge of the dream doesn't help me to control it even though I start to whisper 'tropical island, tropical island'. The words hiss and echo in the empty space and it is off-putting enough for me to stop speaking.

A mint-green plastic curtain separates me from the other half of the room and I don't want to know what is on the other side, but dream-me goes towards it. I am angry and frightened and helpless, unable to make myself wake up or do anything different.

I already know what is behind that curtain because I've dreamed this before. I don't want to see it again.

I watch my hand grip the edge of the curtain and violently cast it aside. The sound of metal rings skittering atop the frame fills my ears as I take in the scene before me.

A heavily pregnant woman is lying on a hospital bed with three people standing around her in bloodstained whites. The effect is both ghastly and ridiculous, for the splatters look better suited for a hack-and-slash movie where characters die one by one.

My mind isn't eased by this comparison.

The faces of the people are easily identifiable. There is Doc Silverbeet, the woman closest to him and assisting is the town vet, Audrey, and the last face is the most familiar because it is my own. It shocks me to have this perspective because I've never watched myself in the scene, I've always been a part of it.

I watch my twin holding one of Samantha's hands in both hers, whispering soothing words of comfort. I don't remember what it is I always tell her. Now that I have a different vantage point, I can see a line of shadowy figures behind each of us, watching.

"Brenda!" Sam screams as a wave of pain hits her and she grabs at her belly. Doc Silverbeet speaks to her, instructing her on what to do and I repeat them until Sam is calm. I notice the shadows have taken a step closer to the bed where she lies and I am horrified that they are getting nearer. They have no right to be in this room. They are unwelcome.

I yell at the shadows, thinking I might shock or surprise the people here but it is more important that the shadows leave than revealing myself. I shouldn't have been worried for the others don't react. They cannot hear me.

The shadows hear me. They have been focussed on Samantha but my voice startles them. I am tense, wondering if they are the ones who are controlling my dream. If they are surprised to see me, is it my own dream? Am I invading some kind of strange, spiritual communication? Is this some kind of twisted recording? Are the shadows watching my memory through my dream?

"Who are you?" I ask. The silhouettes face me. There are no eyes but I sense I am being stared at. "Is it you who bring the lights?"

My question hangs between us and I realise that the scene of the birthing before me has stopped, like someone has hit a pause button. As soon as I identify this however, the scene starts up again with full action and I forget the shadows.

Sam fills the room with her screams and my twin strokes her forehead while holding one of her hands. I move forward and take the other, literally mirroring my twin's movements as the doctors try and rescue my friend and her baby.

Time is skewed by the dream; the birthing takes forever and is over in an instant. When I hear the cries of a baby, I am launched into my twin's body and we merge. The sensation of my two bodies combining is nauseating. Sam calls out for me; the shadows have assembled around her and are doing something that I can't see.

I reach out for Sam but am given a bundle of blankets to hold instead. I look down and uncover the baby's face, only to discover an old-fashioned kewpie doll, with painted eyes and a hideous smile. I look up in confusion at the doctors who are smiling at me.

"Where's the baby?" I ask, showing them the doll. Their smiles change from admiring to quizzical.

"In your arms, Brenda."

"This is a doll!" I insist, thrusting it out to them. Both of them gasp as though I've performed a horrendous act, and Audrey takes the bundle from me as lovingly as a new mother would. I look for Sam but she is no longer on the gurney. The shadows are gone also. I feel as though she might've gone camping to help recover from the birth. Maybe she took the baby? I don't know why she would leave a doll in its place.

"Should I get the father?" Audrey asks Doc Silverbeet.

I look at her with wide eyes.

"Yes, thank you Audrey."

Audrey leaves the room and I try and follow, but she is returning before I get close to the doorway. I worry about the shock the father will feel when he sees the doll that has been swapped for Sam's baby. I can't remember this part of the dream; I don't think I've experienced it before.

When I see whose hand Audrey is holding, I burst out laughing. It sounds hysterical but I am unable to contain myself. The town vet has pulled in a male mannequin.

I awaken with a gasp, sheets clinging to my sweaty skin. My bed looks like I've had a fight with the covers. I don't remember much of the dream other than my idea that Sam had gone camping, leaving her baby behind.

I cover my face with my hands and take deep, measured breaths until I get myself under control. I don't normally dream but I feel my emotional stress has been tested more than usual lately. My subconscious is telling me to get away and that's a piece of advice I won't ignore.

With the decision made, I can relax and I am able to find sleep once more.

I close my eyes and listen to the chirps and gargles of the animals in the bush around me, my face upturned to the sun. When I lower my gaze, I see a wide, sluggish river before me.

I move along the bank, leaving the one person tent I've pitched behind me. The trek is easy enough for I've made it many times before. The destination is both familiar and heartbreaking.

I arrive at the clearing, with a small trio of gums gathered closely together, as if huddling for comfort. The small cairn I've made to mark Sam's grave is still there, untouched. I kneel down before it and make a variant of the same speech I've made since I buried Sam's ashes.

"Samantha," I say, my words already vibrating with the strength of my emotion. "I miss you every day. You called me your rock, but you were that for me. Your daughter is growing up well. Hope is confident and courageous and kind, so kind. You'd be proud of her."

Even while I announce the likelihood of Sam's pride, I wonder if it would be true. She was terrified throughout her pregnancy, her fears transposing to me.

Who was the father of her baby? Did it come from them? Would she give birth to a monster? Would it be some freakish creature? What would she do?

I would allay her fears as best I could, promising that it was unlikely she'd been impregnated by strange creatures.

How do you know? Sam would demand of me. *How* could *you know?*

She was right; how could I know? I am as ignorant as the rest of the town about where we come from and who we are. There have been discussions and speculation, but they have all been made without my input or my presence. I prefer not to talk about what I have no way of changing. I don't want to be riled up by other people's fears. Sam did that to me. I've forgiven her because we had a connection and I loved her with all my heart, but I can't go through that again.

Sam didn't want to go to a hospital for fear of what might come out of her growing belly. Nobody in town insisted, which only seemed to confirm and enhance her fears. She spoke about it to me, explaining that they were happy to risk her pregnancy with a home-birth and a maybe-doctor. Poor Doc Silverbeet hadn't a chance to save Sam, when complication after complication during her pregnancy hit her and we didn't have a full clinic set up. I blamed him, even though he'd saved Hope.

Upon seeing a normal baby, everybody relaxed. Except me.

You are not a forgiving woman, Brenda.

Enzo's words pour into my memory, unbidden and undesired. With a clarity that comes with the passing of time, I understand that I was hurt and angry because his words are true.

I don't forgive. I don't forget. I am a harsh judge and critic.

"I came here to apologise for blaming you, but I can't. You made me suspicious of her, Sam. I can't look at her without thinking of your fear and damn you for doing that, because I want to love her. I want to trust her but I just can't. It was easier when she was a baby. It was easier to dismiss your fears when she was helpless. I kept thinking; what if I'm wrong? What if *you* were wrong? She's just a child... but then she looks at me like she knows what's going on and I--"

I'm terrified of her.

I can't say it out loud. I can't give that thought strength. It's a horrible emotion to suppress and it's one that I'm certain is borne from paranoia. Before he chased the lights and lost his mind, the Doc explained to me that Sam might've been suffering from schizophrenia; except her fears always sounded reasonable to me.

Maybe she'll look normal, Sam told me once, *but she'll be good at everything.*

There are certain truths about Hope that I don't tell Sam's grave.

Hope is extremely advanced for her age. She's intelligent and has a well-rounded personality. She's quick-witted with her humour and is everyone's friend at school. The townsfolk consider her charming and genuine. She's helpful and a hard worker. She's tidy; I don't think I've ever had to ask her to clean up her toys or her room. There are so many examples I have of how she's never tested me or pushed the boundaries like normal children do.

She's not normal.

She's good at everything.

And I am haunted by that.

SECOND LIFE
CHAPTER TWELVE

"I would have liked to go with you," my lover says. We are lying in bed together on one of our lazy late mornings. Popsy is at the Bakery and Hope is in school. This is not the first time he has hinted his displeasure at being left behind while I went camping last week.

"I needed some space."

"From me?"

"From everyone." I find myself disliking his insecurity. I had considered him a confident man and now his questions grate on my nerves. Is it something that I ignored because I was so enchanted with his looks? Am I a shallow woman?

"You can take me with you next time," he says, gesturing at me like I should be making promises. I don't feel like I should offer platitudes.

"I doubt I will, it's a private place."

When he goes quiet I wonder if he's finally accepted my responses. Perhaps I've hurt his feelings. I feel like I'm being awful to him and I take a breath to start offering some time away together—somewhere else. He interrupts a sentence I haven't yet begun.

"You took *Sam*." The name shocks me and I feel my cheeks grow hot. He takes advantage of my silence. "I know that when she died, you haven't been the same. You changed."

"Who have you been talking to?" I ask. "Not Enzo," I say, letting my lover know that the easiest person to point the finger at is not the best, for Enzo would never poison anyone against me.

"Why does it matter who talks when it is true?"

"Because it's none of your business," I say. I pull the sheet up, covering my breasts.

"Why do you push me away?"

"You're in my bed, how am I pushing you away?"

His expression tells me how ridiculous he thinks my argument is. I sigh and look away; I know I'm being defensive but he's asking me about one of my most treasured things. I need something that belongs to me in this town. Everything is shared here. Everybody's actions are watched. I know we are all looking out for one another but I need my space. Sam spoke about getting away from the town so burying her near the campsite seemed the best idea.

"The connection between you and me… why do you think it is so strong?"

I am thrown by this new angle of questioning and hope that he's trying to salvage the romance. I play along willingly.

"Because you're gorgeous and have good

taste," I joke, curling against him. He moves so we can both cuddle together comfortably.

"You don't think we are made for one another?"

I laugh and kiss him. There is a lull in our conversation as our kisses grow heated.

"He let you slip through his fingers," my lover whispers, and kisses me again. I pull back and give him a look that shows my confusion. "His loss, my gain."

"Whose loss? Who are you talking about?"

"Enzo," he says, and chases my lips but I don't allow him to capture them. He pulls back and watches me.

"You've asked me already if we were ever together, and I said no. That was the truth."

"I never said it wasn't, but you were obviously meant to be with him."

"I beg your pardon?" I ask. Talking about Enzo is removing all of my romantic thoughts and I shuffle further away. The sheet is colder at the mattress' edge and it cools my heated skin.

"After Sam died, they gave you Enzo. When you rejected him, *I* came next."

First comes the shock, then comes the anger.

"What the hell are you talking about? I'm not some mindless creation to be pushed about by a bunch of fucking lights!"

He recoils at my volume and blinks his surprise when I swear. He better get used to this part of me, certainly Enzo has, but I don't want to talk about *him* either.

"If you want to be philosophical, you can go to the hall every Friday night for that, but don't accuse me of being anybody's puppet."

"Hey, calm down, I only wanted to—"

"And don't tell me to calm down, like getting angry isn't a normal emotion. You just told me that you feel obligated to be with me, that you're here because of some kind of twisted sense of responsibility and not desire."

"That's not what I said," my lover argues, his tone gentle and reasonable. Right now I want him to show me his passion in a manner beyond sex; otherwise what is he but *their* puppet and what does that make me, falling for a man like him?

"Get out of my bed. Get out of my house."

"Brenda, don't leave it like this. I want to talk it out."

My lover reaches out a hand but I slap it away.

"Do I have to tell you again?" I say, hearing the coldness in my own voice.

He says nothing but I can see his hurt and confusion clearly enough. I feel awful but at the same time I need to be apart from him. I don't think straight when I'm with him; he clouds my judgment. I didn't mean to sleep with him but when he showed up at my door I couldn't resist. Now I am paying for that moment of weakness but he is paying for it more.

I can't watch him as he dresses. He says nothing from the moment he leaves the bed to when he goes out of the door. I listen as the front door opens and shuts.

Even though I'm already aching for him, I'm not going to let anybody influence me or my thoughts again.

SECOND LIFE
CHAPTER THIRTEEN

I am working my way through a pile of books, matching and inserting the on-loan card slips to envelopes taped on the inside front cover. Our library isn't networked or even official; it is more like a second-hand bookstore without charges. Most citizens of Dungoora prefer to read over watching television or listening to the radio. I don't mind the idiot-box, but I always turn off when the news comes on. It is a link to a world I want no part of.

I am crossing Gabriel's name off a card, who likes to read military thrillers, when I am interrupted. The door opens with such ferocity that it slams into the wall panel beside it. One of the library patrons reading near the window, shushes unconsciously. I stare at my lover in disbelief.

"You have to come," he puffs. His eyes are wide and panicked, his hair dishevelled. As I stand, he tells me the reason why. "Popsy."

Popsy is supposed to be working at the bakery.

I leave the library with images of burnt skin and toppling shelves.

"What happened?" I ask as we run together down the footpath.

"I don't know. He fell over."

From his unclear explanation, I deduce my lover has been sent to fetch me and this is why he has no details. By the time we arrive at the bakery there is a throng of people gathered around the door that I have to push past. They don't part for me like I expect and I am annoyed at their curious stares. They are no longer people... they are buzzards.

Two large backs block me and I slam the heels of my hands against them while crying out Popsy's name. It works. They move with an apology and I see Enzo helping to move Popsy onto a makeshift stretcher in the middle of the bakery floor. Audrey is close by as he is lifted and she directs Enzo and his partner as they carry Popsy to the back door, away from the crowd. I join her as she follows them.

"What happened?"

"I can't say so early."

"Then give me your best guess," I say angrily.

"His heart," she says. I follow her outside and watch as Popsy is placed in the back of the van that we use as our makeshift ambulance. "It was bound to happen."

Before she can climb into the front of the ambulance I pull on her arm and she looks at me sadly.

"Bound to? Because he's old?" I ask. I suspect there is more she isn't telling me because of the guilt I can see on her face.

"It's been bothering him a while. He didn't want to worry you." Audrey pulls away and climbs into the front beside her driver.

The words haunt me. It is typical of Popsy to have kept his heart problems a secret. The fact that Audrey is now betraying his wishes tells me how serious his condition is.

My lover joins my side but he says little. Other than fetching me, we have not spoken since I kicked him out of bed last week.

"Did you want me to come with you, to get Hope?" he asks.

I consider refusing his help but it would only spite myself. I nod because Enzo is with Popsy and there is nobody else I want to walk with. My lover and I head towards the school; shoulder to shoulder but not hand in hand.

I speak with Gloria who looks after the kindergarten children. I don't want to cause a scene at Hope's classroom. I doubt I'll be able to call her without tearing up. Being one of their teachers would also lend me more attention than I want right now. I take Gloria's place as she goes to fetch Hope.

There are only three kids to keep an eye on. My lover is immediately accepted by them; they climb all over him as he play wrestles on the floor. When Gloria comes back and Hope joins me, I see confusion on her face. There's no concern, not yet. Her first reaction is never to think of the worst, as I do.

My lover farewells the children and joins us outside, where I struggle to explain what's happened. After a few poor attempts, I finally tell her bluntly.

"Popsy has a heart problem that he didn't want us to worry about and now it's bad."

I can see the shock on her face and her eyes welling with tears. She covers her mouth with her hands and I wonder if she got that habit from me or if it is something hardwired into all people.

"He's going to the hospital to get better," my lover adds, trying to soften the news.

"We don't know that. We should go see him," I say. Perhaps it is cruel to be so harsh, but I don't want to lie to her. There is urgency in me to take her to him, for us to see him before he dies. The idea of his death is both surreal and matter-of-fact in my mind. I can feel both anger and fear battling for my heart.

There is no hospital in town, just the clinic, though it is large with many private rooms. Profits from the petrol station and online trading keeps it well stocked with drugs but we can't seem to save up enough to buy the bigger machines. EBay has been surprisingly helpful for second-hand wheelchairs, cots and even a portable x-ray machine that came with a couple of lead vests.

I know that there are medicines that can help Popsy and I wonder if he has been taking pills in secret. I hope that he has, that he hasn't just left his condition to chance. It would also be like him, to not only keep it a secret but to surrender himself to fate.

The walk to the clinic is made in silence.

Popsy is in a back room, looking pale. There are wires attached to circular pads that link him to a machine that bleeps his heart rate. Audrey moves about the room with a booklet in one hand and an unfamiliar device in the other. Popsy is conscious when we enter and offers Hope a smile. He sees my concern and gives me an awkward shrug. Audrey tells him off for moving and gives me an annoyed look. She knows better than to shoo me out; she tried and failed with Sam years ago. She makes do with shooing away my lover.

"Thank you," I tell him before he goes. He looks back before leaving the room and gives me a smile that both lifts my spirits and pains my heart.

The rest of the day is spent with Popsy as he drifts in and out of consciousness. Audrey monitors him and then researches his symptoms to double-check. It takes her hours before she returns with a suggestion.

"I can't look after him properly here. He'll have more time if he goes to the city." Her words give a great deal away and even though I was braced for bad news, I still have trouble processing it. *More time*, she said, not *a better chance*.

Popsy's eyes were closed but he is awake.

"Home, go home," he says.

Hope leans closer to him.

"Do you want us to go home?" she asks.

"Me," he whispers, his eyelids fluttering.

"Don't exert yourself, Popsy," Audrey says, but her order has no strength to it.

"He wants to go home, Hope. With us." My voice trembles. I'm not ready to lose him.

"But he needs to stay and get better," Hope argues. Her eyes are already glistening. I wonder if she knows. I can't tell her, in case she doesn't.

"Popsy wants his family around him," Audrey says. "I would do as he wishes."

Hope bursts into tears and quickly exits the room. I follow her and hold her. She smothers her sobs against my chest and I feel helpless.

CHAPTER FOURTEEN

I have been holding vigil by his bedside. Popsy looks grey against the stark white pillow and his thin hair is straggly. I want to brush it but don't want to disturb his sleep. I can't help myself; I reach out but snatch my hand back when his eyes open.

"Bunny," he says. His voice is weak but the word is clear.

"Don't talk," I say, concerned about his energy. I don't want him to waste it saying things I don't need to hear.

His expression changes; I recognise the way his brow knits together and his lips press more firmly. He is frustrated with me.

"Unless it's important," I amend. He takes a shallow breath.

"Give me back," he says. I'm confused by what he means and he must see it on my face. "New moon tomorrow… put me in the street. I want… go back."

I am horrified.

"They don't take people back," I argue.

"Sometimes… yes," Popsy says. I reel from the information. Why have I not known this? Samantha didn't go back, nor did she want to. Her ashes remain in the woods, where I buried them.

"Why?" I ask. Popsy doesn't answer. I am torn between not wanting to press him and wanting to know his reason. "Why do you want to go back?"

"It's time. I want to go home."

My vision blurs. I don't understand what he means. This town is his home. Hope and I are his home. Why does he want to be away from us?

Someone's hand touches my shoulder, surprising me, but my only reaction is to swipe it off. Whoever it is can wait for me to be done. Through eyes made hot with tears I realise that Popsy hasn't waited for me — he has passed away.

I feel like I should be sobbing; that I should throw myself on his body and scream my pain, but I can't. I was never that kind of person and I can't be that way now. My chest feels tight and tears streak my cheeks and I summon all of my strength to turn around and look at who is in the room with me. I am expecting my lover but I see Enzo. His face looks gaunt and grey, his appearance mirrors the way I feel inside.

"I'm so sorry," he says to me. His voice betrays the depth of his emotion. As much as I keep my emotions contained within, let out only in private, he is open. Even when he was guarded after my desire for my lover became public knowledge, he was unable to keep his feelings secret. I realise I have always thought of them as his weakness but now I understand that they can be a strength. I know I can trust him and that his words to me are genuine. I stand and my stoicism fades when I feel my face crumple. Enzo steps forward and takes me into his arms and I press myself against him, accepting his comfort.

"Did you hear his request?" I ask into Enzo's chest. His affirmative answer rumbles against my cheek. "I can't just put his body out on the street."

Enzo kisses the top of my head before stepping back from me and holds my upper arms for my attention.

"Don't think of that now. Get Hope."

Enzo lets me go so he can sit on the chair by the bed. I leave him and go downstairs. I find Hope sitting downstairs in front of a silent television, in an armchair adjacent to my lover. They were waiting for me while I had my time with Popsy. I think about the news I have to deliver and know that Hope will be devastated; Popsy was closer to her than I was.

I have my statement ready but I don't need it because as soon as Hope looks my way she bursts into tears. She covers up her face and pulls her feet up, huddling in a ball on the cushion. I hurry to her and sit beside her, enveloping her in my arms. I am apprehensive until she leans against me, unresisting. As I have allowed Enzo to comfort me, she has allowed me to do it for her. Taking his cue, I kiss the top of her head and am glad when she reaches an arm around my middle to cling to me.

"Would you like to go see him?" I ask. Over her head I make eye contact with my lover before he breaks it by lowering his gaze to his lap. I can almost feel his discomfort at invading Hope's grief.

Hope answers not with words but with a nod and so I stand to help her to her feet. I ask if she wants me to go with her and she declines with a shake of the head. She goes upstairs and I am left with my lover who eventually lifts his gaze to meet mine.

"Will you bury him in the forest, too?" he asks. The question feels harsh and heartless in the moment of loss. I can tell by his tone that he has not meant it this way but the words cause me to look away, my eyes stinging. Unlike Enzo, he doesn't collect me into his arms to soothe my pain but speaks instead. "Do you not do that with the ones you love?"

"He wants to go home," I say, and I choose not to clarify Popsy's request to my lover who looks at me quizzically. He doesn't ask me any further questions and so we wait in silence, listening to the brief sounds upstairs as Enzo and Hope mourn Popsy's passing by his bedside.

CHAPTER FIFTEEN

The funeral service goes by in a blur. I stand behind the podium, feeling uncomfortable with the casket at my back. There is a scribbled note that I read from, but I don't remember writing it and it makes no sense even as I read it. It is like I am speaking another language, living in another time. After I finish speaking I stare at the room full of faces and think about how strange they all look. Enzo stands and collects me, leading me back to my seat.

The service is over soon afterward and Enzo continues to look after me with an arm around my shoulders. I look through the crowd and finally see my lover's face. He is with a couple of the older townsfolk but he is not being his usual charming self. I can tell by his downcast mouth. He looks towards me and I avert my gaze.

Hope clings to Enzo's other hand, younger and smaller than I remember. I feel sorry for her, because now all she has left is me.

As if she has heard my thought, Hope looks at

me with pleading eyes.

"Can I stay with Enzo tonight?"

I want to ask her why. I want to point out that Enzo will be one of the people that are laying Popsy's body out on the street for collection. I don't want her to see that.

"Of course you can." Enzo answers for me and I look at him. His hand upon my shoulder gives a brief rub. Perhaps he feels I need my space and his taking Hope from me will make me feel better. I want to confront him and explain that Hope should be with me; tonight of all nights… but I can't. She wants to be with Enzo and I don't want to give her more reasons to hate me.

Enzo leans closer to me and I tip my head to accommodate his lips near my ear. "I'll send him around to your place."

Him? Of course I know he means my lover. He thinks that the two of us are still exploring our new romance. Why would he believe anything different? I've said nothing and obviously my lover hasn't either.

Thinking of him, I look his way and catch him staring. He offers me a smile but I don't have one in me to return. I toy with the idea that I am in shock, but it doesn't feel like I expected it would. Shock is supposed to sweep every thought out of one's head, surely? I feel like there are too many in mine.

There will be a wake held at my neighbour's across the street but I decline with a shake of my head. I register expressions of pity around me but I don't care. They can feel sorry for me if they want to. It doesn't change anything.

Peripherally I see my lover heading towards

me. I hurriedly make an excuse and leave the hall. I don't know if I want him to hurry after me or leave me alone but I make it home without interruption. With my heart in my throat I lunge through the door and slam it shut behind me where I crumple onto the floor. I force myself to take deep breaths until I feel calmer. I expect someone will knock on my door.

Nobody does.

SECOND LIFE
CHAPTER SIXTEEN

I am calm at dusk when I watch the procession move along the street. Popsy's body is wrapped in a sheet. I think about the open casket back at the hall where his service was held earlier today. What will happen to it? I don't know why I am thinking about it.

I see Enzo is one of the men carrying Popsy's body. There are two of them holding him in a way that looks strange to me. They are carrying him as though he sits on a chair between them. I imagine if he were alive he'd have each of his arms extended upon their shoulders. The idea gives me a chill and I fold my arms across my chest, holding my own upper arms. I feel goosebumps on my skin.

Popsy's wrapped body is laid in the middle of the street in front of my house. I have a strong sensation that it will still be there tomorrow morning and that we will be forced to preserve it, so that we can put his body out on the street every new moon until they come to take it away.

If they come and don't take it away, we will know that we will have to do something different. There is a cemetery but Popsy's request makes me think that he doesn't want to go there. I think of Sam's grave in the woods but that was a special place to her as much as to me. The only places I know of that were special to Popsy were this house and the bakery. I doubt his final resting place will be at either of those locations.

Maybe they will come. Maybe they will take his body away, like he thought they would. I hope they do.

I can hear Enzo's voice speaking softly over Popsy's body. The other man is Logan who worked with Popsy at the bakery. They both have their heads down, as though they are praying. I've never known Enzo to pray, or anyone else in town.

Maybe we feel we have no souls to save.

The men step away. Logan and Enzo walk in opposite directions; Logan to a house that he shares with his wife and baby son, and Enzo to a house that has my lover and Hope in it.

Enzo sees me standing on the porch and raises a hand to wave. I lift mine in return and he continues on. Even though night-time is fast approaching, I can easily see the shape of Popsy's shrouded body in the street. I can't bear to look at it but at the same time I don't want to look away.

"Goodbye, Popsy. I love you."

I go inside the house because there is nothing for me to see out here. I will only punish myself by staring at the shell of an old man who I loved dearly.

By now I should expect to be joined by my

lover but he must have made an excuse not to come because nobody arrives at my door. I make a tea for myself and sit at the kitchen table. I can hear the radio in the next room playing the kind of music Popsy liked best. The pack of cards nearby beckons me and I gather them up to play solitaire with. It is a mindless task and I have no idea if I've played ten or twenty or fifty times before the hairs on my nape prickle.

The vibrations begin. My eyes widen as I realise the radio is still on and I've left everything plugged in. Cards slide across the table and some fall to the floor as I leave my seat hurriedly. I switch off the kitchen light and enter the sitting room but I am too late. I move through the doorway just in time to hear feedback and see sparks flying out of the radio. I cry out and cover my eyes but I am far enough away from it that my instinct was unnecessary.

I hear them coming; the screamers.

I run around the dark house, pulling everything from the outlets. It is only a safety precaution; things only blow up if they're turned on, not if they're plugged in. The desire to stick to routine remains. The last thing I unplug is the kettle as the last screamer goes past my house.

I race to the window and peer out. It is very hard to see anything but I am sure the dark mound in the middle of the street is Popsy's body. What else could it be? He is still there. I don't know whether to be excited or anxious that they have come again so soon. I don't know whether I want them to take him or not.

The house shudders and for the first time I

think I can hear the blue light before I see it. The note must be very low and very loud to make the house vibrate this way, but my ears aren't reacting to sound. Perhaps I am feeling, not hearing.

The street is washed with blue and the white shroud that Popsy is wrapped in possesses an almost neon glow. I press my hand to my mouth to stop myself from crying out. I want to shout at them to leave him alone, but it is his wish to go to them. I must not interfere.

The blue light doesn't seem to be moving along as quickly as usual. I crouch at the window, to look up at the sky. I can't see very well because of the overhanging roof over the porch. For a good view I would need to step outside.

Nobody steps outside. I hear even the Doc cowers.

The blue light leaves and I can't see anything but black outside. While I wait for my eyes to grow accustomed to the lack of light, I can see the bouncing torchlights.

The old fear returns and I move aside, pressing my back to the wall beside the window. My courage to see what happens to Popsy's body fails me and my mind fills with justifications; I don't need to see them take him, they might not anyway, his body will be there for me to find in the morning.

I yelp and press my hands to my mouth when two circles of light penetrate the window and search the far wall. I watch them dance around one another and then a third spot joins them. I whisper a mantra to myself: "Go away, go away, go away, go away," and wait for them to heed my wish.

All three of them move in unison, leaving my kitchen and me to my pounding heart. I want to look out the window but the idea of doing so makes me feel like I need the toilet. I am so scared. I don't remember ever being this scared.

There is no noise, the animals are still quiet but I feel as though the lights have moved on. The sensation of them going persists for long enough that I can gather my courage and peek out the window.

I can make out the street and the line of the house across from mine. I can't see Popsy's body.

He's gone.

"NO!"

The scream is not mine but it is familiar. I am momentarily stunned with the realisation that Popsy was right, they *did* take him away. I don't recognise Hope's voice because I don't normally hear it raised in such a way.

I recognise Enzo's voice next, though.

"Hope! No!"

I look out the window and I see someone running down the street towards the fields. The fields are where the torchlights always go. They come from the bush and go to the fields, that's a constant.

I see clearly that the running figure is Enzo, and I know why he is going there. I don't have time to think beyond that knowledge, I am out the door and down the porch stairs. As I pass Enzo's house I realise why I could see him; the porch light is blazing.

My darling Hope. My lovely Hope has gone after the lights, to stop them from taking Popsy away. My wonderful Hope, whose shining smile lifts the town's spirits, whose clever observations makes us all proud. She risks her mind to save a corpse because she loved him.

I have already caught up to Enzo and am passing him. He doesn't call out my name because he wants me to get her. We both love her. We both want more for her.

The air is crisp and coldest on my cheeks where my tears have streaked. We are in the fields. Hope is ahead of me, her hair streaming. She is close to the torchlights and this urges me to find an extra touch of power in my sprint, my legs carrying me faster than I thought capable. As her form disappears into the black, my foot lands awkwardly on a furrow and I am launched forward. I am winded; I both hear and feel my breath leave my body in one stunned cough before sliding upon unyielding earth, grazing skin and tasting clumps of dried grass. For a moment I am still, taking stock of where I am most pained before I struggle onto all fours, adrenalin fuelling my actions. I manage to push myself upright and kneel tall. It is in this position that the torchlights find my face and hold me in position. I am unable to move.

I can't see anything except the source. Everything else is black and I understand that I am allowed to communicate with them. I wonder if this is something I've invented, this knowledge, and then the sensation repeats itself; *I know*. This is the way they speak with one another, how they share ideas and emotions. I have been invited into their circle. I understand that there are many questions they are willing to answer for me, but the most important request I make is the one that escapes my lips.

"I want her back," I sob, my voice trembling. There is no strength to my words because I can barely draw breath. My weak demand feels inconsequential in the cool night air.

They understand my desire but they translate her feelings for me. I am awash with Hope's rejection and abandonment. I am surprised to find these emotions are not because of me but are connected to Popsy's death. When it comes to me, Hope is mostly confused and upset that I haven't partnered with Enzo, who she knows loves both her and me and wants to be a father to her. I have made her life difficult by accepting a man she doesn't know and rejecting one that is important to her.

I am shocked at the dilemma she has presented me and I know that they have passed on my reaction to her. I am aware how open and emotional this manner of communication is and that there is nowhere to hide. My secrets are no longer applicable, nor desirable, if I want Hope's trust.

And then they connect me to the love she has for me. It is so strong that I can't think beyond it; my heart aches with the weight of the emotion and the acceptance she has of me. While I have worried about who she is and where she comes from, she has loved and accepted me. Every small gesture of rejection I've let slip in her presence, she has interpreted as caring. As I react against her calling me her mother, she thinks it is because I don't wish to steal the memory of her real mother from her;

memories that only I can relay to her because she has none of her own. She believes my actions come from nowhere except from love and has accepted my inner struggles as shows of strength.

To know such things would cause me to despise myself but to feel the purity of the love she has for me... it decimates my self-worth. I don't deserve her but I still want her back. Now more than ever. I sense that I will never know if she is part of them or all of us, but I no longer care.

When faced with such emotion, I would be a monster to ignore it.

"Give... her... back."

I am aware that they are now shielding their communication from me. I am allowed to know they are discussing whether or not I deserve her. My heart becomes icy in my chest and I moan. I think about what Hope wants and wonder if they'll let her decide.

I can feel the cold mud on my legs as I await their decision and squint against the lights still trained on my face. They are determined not to let me see them. I don't know if they have corporeal bodies. I don't know how they're stopping me from using my own.

Instead of being given an answer, I am asked if I genuinely want to know who and what she is. Do I need this knowledge before I'll accept her?

The gravity of the sentiment has me unable to think a coherent sentence. The emotions that I send to them are answer enough; pain and guilt and shame. I am glad that they communicate with their emotions for I could not translate what I'm feeling into words if I tried.

The idea of never seeing her again would haunt me beyond Popsy's death, beyond Sam's death. I was a fool to keep her at a distance when she'd already been taken into my heart. I am amazed and impressed and grateful that I haven't ruined her with my inability to trust.

So I can trust her now.

No.

I can feel them checking my mind, to see if my emotions are marrying up with my answer. I can feel their satisfaction and their decision to reward me. I wait for Hope to come to me but something else happens instead.

Deep within I understand that they have shared this information in the past. I understand that the Doc begged them for answers that his mind wasn't able to cope with. They sense from me that I need answers. I have a moment to fear for my sanity when the truth is revealed.

We have all died.

I struggle to make sense of the information. In this world we have perished; either by accident or purposefully. They show me a memory that looks like video footage of a handsome man who continually addresses the camera. I am made to understand that I was in a relationship with this man; but he is someone I don't recognise or have any feelings for.

I see anger in his face. I see a knife in his hand. I see the blade rise and fall, getting bloodier with every motion. I see pain and disgust in his face as he takes my life. The story is clear and tragic and I am unable to hide my dismay. It is a strange feeling to see myself playing a role in a movie I don't recall. A movie that is supposed to have been my reality.

Nothing else makes sense after that; just a lot of second-hand imagery through eyes that don't feel human and knowledge that defies me. The science is too abstract and the closest my mind can make of it is that I am some kind of clone. 'Clone' is the wrong association though. It is more as though we have risen from the dead, and the process gives us new, fresh bodies. I understand that the woman I am now is the same woman who was murdered back then. I am not a copy of her—somehow I *am* the original. It is a science so beyond my understanding, it feels like magic.

"Hope," I murmur, both asking about her and requesting her return.

I am shown Samantha's memories. Did they misinterpret or am I meant to see this? A bridge with weeds growing through concrete. The broken rail that shows a long fall to rocks below. I don't need to see anymore to understand what happened. The imagery goes as soon as I resist it. Was she pregnant when she chose to jump? I assume so—I can't know what she was thinking.

Doc's words make a horrible sense. *Sam wanted to be dead. No Hope for that one.* He wasn't responsible for her death, he wasn't trying to tell me he sacrificed her to save the baby. He talked to the lights too.

They ask if I want to know more and I can't help but summon my lover's face.

His imagery contains a great deal of flashing blue, red and orange. There is an overturned truck that has some kind of chemical spill and ahead of him there are fire fighters running towards their truck while he runs to a police cruiser. Is my lover a policeman? It certainly explains a lot. The scene disappears into white and then orange and I understand that he perished in a massive roadside explosion.

I think of Enzo next but as soon as I do, I feel his protest in my mind. He doesn't want me to know how he died and he doesn't want to know for himself either. I realise that I have been connected with Enzo this whole time though I hadn't felt him until now. Is he nearby? Did the lights gather his thoughts the same time they gathered mine? His protest is apparently not as important as my curiosity, because I am shown.

I see a young woman with a beautiful smile and sad eyes. She is looking down at me and caressing my forehead. The room we are in looks to be in a hospital. She moves away and comes back, wearing a different outfit. I watch her gradually age; there are more wrinkles around her eyes and mouth and the painted hospital walls become floral wallpaper. The illness was a long one. Enzo's wife remained with him until the end.

The rest of us died quickly and violently, but Enzo was different. I don't know how I feel about it when the memory is taken away but I *can* feel Enzo's desire to learn more.

I am questioned about what I will do with all of this knowledge. I don't have to say anything; the answer is deep within my psyche and they can clearly see my strong opinion.

I will keep it to myself.

Like them, I understand that not everybody in

town will be able to cope with such knowledge. I fear that they might decide to look for the loved ones that their deaths may have left behind — or revenge, in my case. It would lead to the discovery of the town and our lives would change

Enzo disagrees. He wants the townsfolk to learn the truth and make their own decision. He isn't comfortable deciding for them. I argue that his choice would be taking the option away from those who would prefer to live an untainted life. Discovery cannot be undone or ignored. He is moved by my response but remains frustratingly stubborn.

My next thought manages to sway him; the lights would stop coming. There will be no more second chances. No more second lives. I don't want to ruin it for others. If we wish to continue as we are, the secret must be kept. I can feel his sense of obligation warring with his moral righteousness but they confirm my prediction. There will be no more lights. They will stop.

Within me I feel Enzo balk at this. He grudgingly relents; he will keep his silence, but he wants to know why. Why have the lights come? Why are they doing this? What do they want?

We are an experiment. I have always considered this but it is one thing to imagine and quite another to know. The knowledge arrives with a sensation of elitism — we are thought of as lesser species with promise. A word comes to my mind that sums up their assessment; we have *potential*. They wanted to know what lay at the core of a human being. They removed our memories but not the understanding of civilisation. Instead of being hostile to one another, we built a better, peaceful variant for ourselves. Our lack of memories bonded us. They were proud of us when we helped one another and welcomed each stranger into the community. As much as I am glad they look upon us affectionately, I dislike the sensation of superiority that I am getting with it.

I no longer want to be a part of this. There is only one thing I want.

"Give me back my daughter," I say, hearing the slur in my voice. It is getting harder to speak as I grow used to being a part of their network.

I am scared by a sudden suspension of knowledge. I don't know what anybody is thinking or feeling anymore. I begin to sway and I'm feeling lost and alone. Have I been disconnected?

"Hope!" I sob into the darkness, for the torchlight has left my face. I am blinded by a lack of light, seeing after-glow everywhere I look. I crawl on hands and knees when I hear footsteps running towards me. I am disoriented; I don't know if they are behind me (Enzo?) or in front of me (Hope?).

A weight hits me from in front; small arms reach around me and I am overwhelmed by the smell of Hope's shampoo. I can't say her name, my throat is clogged with emotion. I choke in gasps of breath and release my sobs. I am crying because I have my girl in my arms; my Hope, and the reason why my second life has had any meaning at all.

SECOND LIFE
CHAPTER SEVENTEEN

It will take me a long time to forgive myself, if ever, for keeping her at a distance. I have already lost many years as Hope's caring, loving mother—but it would be fallacy to lose more while grieving for what was lost. This time I am determined to look forward and not back.

I have allowed myself to accept love. I have allowed myself to show love in return. I have allowed myself to be happy. I am holding hands with my loved ones. Hope stands on one side, and my Romeo on the other. The name my lover chose for himself was one I scoffed at, but it suits him and I am getting used to it.

I watch Enzo loading the back of his ute. Gabriel is now responsible for driving into the city and getting the town's weekly perishable supplies because Enzo is leaving.

I worry for him, that Enzo will seek out the woman who loved him. I worry that he won't find her. I worry more that he will.

Enzo has agreed not to destroy our community and I trust that he will protect us and our secret. He loves me and I love him, but not in the way he wanted me to. He knows that now and has come to terms with it. Or perhaps he hasn't and that is why he wants to go.

I will miss him and I wish for him the best outcome. I have managed to find the best for myself; living with both of my loved ones, smiling and laughing with them. I know things about them that they will never know and I am at peace with that.

I think Enzo's heart feels weighed down by the knowledge given him... and that is where we misalign the most, for I needed the truth to set my heart free.

FORTUNE

"There are two clear paths," the fortune-teller says. My sister's fingers twitch upon my arm. We're both believers of pre-determined destiny, ever since the accident. "In one, you will live with beauty in the dark, and in the other, brutality in the light."

My sister gasps and I can sense she's horrified with my choices. I'm not so adversely affected. I'd accept a thousand brutalities, if only to see again. I'm already living with the ultimate brutality, as an artist gone blind.

I'd been invited to participate in a high profile gallery showing of emerging young painters. I'd been interviewed, written about, my paintings and my name attracting the kind of attention that budding artists usually dream about. Success in my world was rare, especially at twenty-five.

That was ten years ago. My mother and sister had wanted to share in my success. They'd flown to Sydney with me, and at the airport we'd been waiting in the queue as taxis picked up passengers ahead of us. A stern looking middle-aged man lined up and almost immediately grabbed my wrist.

"There will be other opportunities," he'd said, wide-eyed and unyielding in his grip when I tried to tug my hand away. At first I'd been too shocked to make a sound, so he was able to continue his warning. "Go back home, or you'll never paint again."

He was crazy. I found my voice and yelled at him to let me go. He released me and left when my mother and sister pitched in. We'd spent the next few minutes in line complaining and then laughing about how weird everybody in Sydney was. Even with the jokes we'd made, I'd been unsettled by his claim.

He was right. The taxi crashed and the driver was instantly killed. My mother, riding in the front, died in the ambulance on the way to the hospital. I was knocked unconscious and upon waking, saw nothing but blackness. My sister escaped unscathed, and lives with immeasurable guilt. She supresses that guilt by assisting me.

"What kind of brutality?" I ask, and receive silence. My sister tells me I've earned a shrug.

"I see nothing more," the fortune-teller says, and I ponder her inappropriate choice of words.

Two months later I'm part of a medical trial for a new kind of drug that may restore my vision. There have been many arguments with my sister, who insists I shouldn't participate in case I attract the kind of brutality I've been warned about.

I ignore her. She doesn't understand the kind

of horror I face every day. She talks of opportunity and growth, of coping and finding new hobbies to satisfy myself with. Painting is not a hobby, it is my life, and I lost it when I lost my sight. She is just a model. She is an object of beauty, not a creator of it.

The last stage of the trial requires my placement into a medical coma. My sister's hand is not the one that guides mine to the required locations on the forms. I sign my consent with flourished practise. My head and my heart pound with hope.

In the coma I find peace. There are no thoughts or worries, just the blackness that I am familiar with and resent. I am unconscious so I don't notice it. When the need arises, I am awakened.

I open my eyes.

Everything is white.

DOT MATRIX

"What's that sound?" George Griper asked, turning in a half circle so he could better look down the sparse surgical corridor. The smell of the place reminded him of a hospital, but there was an undercurrent of chemicals that didn't belong. Like sulphur. He adjusted his gold-rimmed glasses in a fruitless attempt to see something more than frosty-blue painted walls. The noise was unsettlingly familiar, yet made no sense in a place like this.

"Oh, that's just the printers, they run non-stop," came the nasal response. The woman who was his tour guide was one Dr Bernadette McKellar, whose notoriety in her chosen field of bioengineering was a great deal more inspiring than her non-descript physical appearance. She wasn't unattractive; she was just bland, like over-steamed beans.

"They sound like..." he struggled for the specific noun, but couldn't remember it, "... old-fashioned printers," he finished lamely, dissatisfied with his description and also with Dr McKellar's inability to interject with the correct word.

"Dot matrix printers," she supplied, revealing that she'd known the words he was after. He pressed his lips tightly together, feeling his own discontent thrumming through his body and echoing in his expression. The doctor either didn't notice or chose to ignore it. "It's the last part of our tour," she said, and there was a new quality to her tone that caught his attention. He didn't know her well enough to interpret it correctly, but if he was forced to hazard a guess, he might go so far as to call it excitement. They began walking down the corridor towards the sound. His shoes clicked on the laminate floor while hers squelched.

"Dot matrix printers?" he repeated, though he'd heard the words clearly and now that the sound was identified, it was obvious. How could he have struggled to place it before?

"We find they produce the best results," Dr McKellar said. George glanced at her, wondering if she was being facetious, but her profile was impassive. She was declaring a fact, as she'd been doing throughout the tour. She used unemotional language and spoke in riddles, because it flowed from her thoughts rather than from the conversation. Many times today he'd been forced to ask for clarification, and it seemed the present moment was no exception.

"The best results for what?" he asked, and adjusted his glasses again.

"Respectfully, Mr Griper, I believe this is something best seen yourself."

He frowned but politely obeyed her suggestion and didn't ask further questions. As they walked along the corridor, the chattering of the printers grew louder, and he began to feel like the protagonist in a horror story, advancing towards his own death. In this case, eaten alive by a swarm of electronic locusts. The noise was maddening, and they hadn't yet stepped into the room.

They stopped at a door and as Dr McKellar reached for the I.D. card attached to the lanyard she wore about her neck, George was aware of another sound beneath the squalling printers. It was a number of high octave beeps that followed a rhythm, though an unusual one. This time he recognised it as medical equipment, but as the card was swiped and the door unlocked with a click, he still wasn't ready to understand what he was looking at when the door was pushed open.

The doctor moved through the doorway without hesitation, and George followed her through it, looking to his left because that was where the beds, machines and bodies were. He could smell something different in this room that he hadn't perceived out in the corridor. It was a gentle smell but certainly one he associated with hospitals.

"Centrimide," she said, still walking further into the room.

"I beg pardon?"

"It's the disinfectant you can smell," she said, and stopped at the fourth and last bed in order to turn around and look at George directly. He blinked at her, wondering how she could've known his thoughts when she hadn't even been looking in his direction. Was it a common question when people were shown in here?

He acknowledged her comment with a nod and then looked closer at the person lying upon the bed closest to the door. A woman, though this was difficult to make out thanks to the oxygen mask over her face and the multitude of wires that were suction cupped to her torso. It was her small frame and breasts that gave her away, for the sheet only covered her up to the waist. There were even a few wires snaking out from under the sheet on her lower half, but the real focus seemed to be at her chest. There were a number of differently coloured wires that ran from the woman's upper body and plugged into two small grey boxes on stands either side of the bed. A quick glance revealed that each person was hooked up the same way. A large machine pumped oxygen beside the bed, and it was this machine that unsettled him the most.

"I thought you didn't perform live experiments?" he asked, trying not to sound as alarmed as he felt.

"We don't. They're brain-dead."

Her answer didn't settle his uneasiness, and he couldn't help but look her way. He was surprised to see a somewhat vacant expression; he'd genuinely expected to see a Mona Lisa secretive smile at best, or one of predatory interest at worst. His stare found the woman on the bed once more. She fascinated him.

Is this even legal? He wanted to shriek at her, but his professionalism took hold.

"Did they donate their bodies towards scientific research?" he asked, pleased that he sounded a great deal calmer than he felt. Now Dr McKellar sounded amused.

"Of course. We're keeping them as comfortable as possible. All of their requests are immediately met." Her answer rewarded her his attention once more.

"I beg your pardon. All of their requests?"

"Yes," she replied, and swept her arm like a 60's game-show hostess to the dot matrix printers opposite the beds. George followed her gesture and watched them run. From this distance he saw nothing but a series of lines, so he moved closer in order to peer at the paper feed.

It was the kind of output one might expect to get if a thousand monkeys typed on a thousand keyboards for a thousand years – and it wasn't Shakespeare. It wasn't even a constant series of letters, it included jumbles of symbols; hashes and at signs, percentages and numbers, asterisks and brackets. There were letters in the mix too, but they were lost amongst the mess.

He was good at making connections, and he suspected where the output was coming from, though he didn't know how or why. His gaze followed the cords that came out of the printer and ran up the wall – attached to it with a series of metal clips – and then along the ceiling and back down the opposite wall, near the beds, where they were almost lost in a network of wires and other plugs, but George managed to make out the data plug connected into the anonymous grey box at her bedside.

He looked back at the doctor who was watching him and felt the need to confirm what he was seeing.

"The woman is attached to the box, and the box runs the printer."

"Yes."

He thought about that for a moment.

"The output for the printer is coming from the box."

"No," she replied, and squelched closer to him.

"It can't come from her when she's brain dead," he argued, and took a step back. Dr McKellar stopped where she was and gave him a poor attempt of a comforting smile.

"It's not coming from her brain," she said gently, speaking to him as though he were a small child.

No, George thought spitefully, it's coming from the box. What trickery is this?

"You're using her as a battery!" he sputtered, feeling the need to remain hostile and offended, but unsure why. This unknowing fed his animosity further.

"I assure you this project isn't so simplistic," she said, and now there was an edge to her voice he hadn't heard before. He lifted his chin triumphantly as she continued. "Look at her printout with me, if you please," she instructed, and moved over to it. He followed and watched as the doctor produced a fluorescent marker out of her lab coat pocket and searched for something to highlight for him. She found it after a moment, then again after a little more searching. At first he couldn't identify what he was looking at, because it wasn't a word. When she highlighted a third one, he saw the repetition of symbols. Two hyphens, an apostrophe, two hyphens, a comma, two more hyphens, a left brace and an at sign.

--'--,--{@

"That's… that's…" he said, once again losing the word he was looking for.

"An ASCII art rose," she provided, taking the cue this time.

"But…"

He had nothing to finish his sentence with, and the doctor waited him out for a very long moment before she decided he was finished.

"This subject is the most extraordinary example we've come across yet. Unlike the others, which produce a word or even a phrase from time to time, have never repeated something in a way that proves without doubt that there is more to memory than we would normally believe. Her first name was Rose, she was named after her grandmother who kept an expansive rose garden in a small greenhouse in her backyard. She worked as a florist. She died of a brain embolism while making a delivery to a woman in hospital. The woman's husband had purchased a dozen red roses for her."

He boggled at Dr McKellar and she smiled back.

"So she's not dead!" he cried.

"Oh, she most certainly is."

"But how can you say that after looking at this?" he challenged.

"It's just feedback," she said, like he should've drawn this conclusion himself. "If I hooked you up to this machine, you'd be able to communicate quite effectively through it. What we're doing here is mapping memory currents."

But what if you're wrong? George thought as they stared at one another. This time her features didn't seem so ordinary, so bland. His new perception of her painted her as a shrewd, heartless creature. Maybe she'd botoxed her forehead so that her maniacal expressions wouldn't give her away. This was something out of science fiction, yes? This was the kind of room that would inspire a mad scientist to take over the world with an army of purpose-built zombies.

"Well, I thank you for this tour, Doctor. Is this the last stop?"

His voice was calm to his own ears, but there was an odd pause as the doctor studied him. She must have been satisfied with what she found.

"Yes, Mr Griper. Will we be receiving a copy of your report?"

"Most certainly," he said with a nod, his words breathless and rushed.

He was glad to turn away from that stare, gladder still to put the research centre in his rear-view mirror. As he steered his car down the long driveway that was in fact a private road, he thought about the woman. Rose. She was a 'specimen', and her 'output' was 'feedback'. Her cries for recognition and acknowledgement were circled in yellow fluorescent marker and filed away to be studied.

And all he could do was write an accounting report.

AIR FIRE WATER EARTH
AIR

I thought it would be silent, but the wind roars in my ears. My hair streams behind me, like a model at a photo-shoot. My clothing flaps noisily and I marvel at how cold I feel. I didn't expect it to be this chilly in the middle of summer.

People jump out of planes and off buildings for a thrill, but I feel calm and at peace. I wonder if their rush comes from their gamble of safety. Are they concerned their parachute won't open? Do they think they're plummeting to their death? Is that where the thrill comes from? Fear? I don't understand why they would be drawn to this, if this is the case.

I don't worry about whether my chute will open, or if some harm will come to me. My eyes are open, figuratively speaking, because right now my eyes are screwed tightly shut. The wind is hurting them as I plunge toward the earth.

I open them now because I need to see. I don't have goggles. I don't have those baggy onesies that the professionals wear. I don't have a parachute.

The ground rushes up faster than I expected, and my last thought is one of surprise.

FIRE

The crackle of flames warms my skin and I feel it tighten in response. It is not a pleasant sensation so I move further back.

The fire before me spits like a hostile animal, yet it moves fluidly like water. How can opposites be so similar? I've read somewhere that water is the strongest element because it can erode anything given enough time. I disagree; the fire before me draws the water out of my body and hot air parches my throat.

I make my way to the window. It has become a gaping space without glass. With nowhere to go I turn and watch as papers catch alight and flutter through the air. The fire gains strength as it eats a path towards me. Acrid smoke plumes and sends blind, seeking fingers along the ceiling. The wind at this altitude is strong and it saves me from choking.

I have a decision to make as the fire corners me. The screams of pain uttered by my co-workers make my choice clear. The fact of death remains, it's the mystery of the making that propels me to the edge.

There are those that cannot bring themselves to jump. I am not one of them.

WATER

I can't breathe. Everything is dark. I am aware of lying in a strange position; my arm is pinned above my head and my wrist is aching. I can't move at all. The cloying sensation of rising panic threatens to overwhelm me but I know it won't help. I cry out but I can hear other people screaming in fear and in pain. My voice blends in with theirs so I stop.

My eyes have adjusted to the darkness and now I can see a glimpse of light. I shuffle and kick my feet simultaneously and I feel something shift off my legs. More shuffling and kicking dislodges a weight from my chest. I can now move one of my arms and I shove debris off myself.

When I climb out of the wreckage, I am stunned by what I see. The place where I work looks like it's been hit by a bomb. Water is gushing into the open-plan offices from the floor above. Sparks are zapping from beside the photocopier and I have just enough time to realise the danger of it when a flare of light explodes from the machine. I am not standing in a puddle of water but most of my co-workers are. They are launched off their feet like movie stunt-doubles off trampolines, except there is no entertainment here. Only death.

Hot coffee leaps out of my cup and splashes over my wrist. I am pitched to one side and smack my shin against a partition wall before it topples over. I notice the stain of spilt coffee on the carpet and wonder if I can get it out.

A desk is doing the hula and a typist chair spins a pirouette. This impromptu dance hall is filled with furniture, punctuated by the odd shriek. I cradle my hurting hand against my chest and crawl awkwardly to take cover from falling ceiling panels.

I can hear someone issuing orders but the voice is distant and irrelevant. My ears are filled with rumbling and my mind struggles to make sense of what I'm seeing.

The earthquake has made the building come alive; the walls are breathing in and out and I feel trapped in the belly of a concrete monster. Lights and computer monitors sputter their discontent as one by one they grow dark, consumed by the beast.

Two people are cramped in the nook beneath the closest desk. Their faces belong to friends but their expressions make them strangers. I continue to the next desk but I am unable to reach it before the ceiling lets out a huge crack and half of the floor above descends upon me.

My eyes close as the darkness becomes complete.

CREATIONISM

Both 'Creationism' and 'Love of Country' were written for two separate teams that were participating in 2014 GISHWHES (the Greatest International Scavenger Hunt the World Has Ever Seen). The story had to be penned by a science fiction author, be 140 words or less and contain the following elements: Misha Collins (actor and founder of GISHWHES), the Queen of England and an elopus (an elephant/octopus hybrid that was the 2014 mascot).

"Would you like some tea?"

The Queen of England enters the laboratory with a toy teapot filled with water. She finds a beaker and sits on the floor with her legs akimbo.

"I'm busy!" her re-animator spits without looking her way. "Play with Misha."

"He's playing superheroes."

The scientist doesn't consider either of them a

success. They are not creations, they are re-animations. Their second chance at life is filled with simplicities like tea-parties and dress-ups.

A thrown switch fills the laboratory with a hum; bottles shake, lights flicker and the Queen's beaker explodes. She tsks and looks for another vessel.

"It's alive!" he screams, watching tentacles quiver.

"Would it like some tea?" the Queen asks as she tips water onto the Elopus. Wires fizzle and sparks fly.

A caped Misha enters the lab.

"Yummy! Calamari for lunch!"

LOVE OF COUNTRY

The phone shrills. Its high pitched gargle demands my attention. I bark into the mouthpiece; "Who wants pizza?"

"The Queen of England," is the prompt reply. My thoughts tumble, spilling into nonsense.

"Where?" I breathe.

I receive co-ordinates and commit them to memory. There is a click before the pitch of a dial-tone haunts my ear.

The co-ordinates take me to a man on the beach. He is holding a grease-stained pizza box and my stomach grumbles.

"Who are you?" I ask.

"Misha," he replies, and gestures at my empty hands. I shrug.

A grey periscope appears before a hulking

body slithers out of the waves. The creature is a hybrid; part elephant, part octopus. An Elopus. It gulps down Misha's pizza and trumpets its discontent at me before returning to the ocean.

I have let my country down.

MECCA

Her hair fanned out on the pillow like a golden halo. She smiled at him and he dutifully smiled back.

"What was it like for you as a boy?" she asked. He shook his head, she didn't want to hear stories of bitterness and pain, but it was ingrained in him to do as a woman asked, so he told her about a more innocent time, when he was eight.

The young boy flattened his nose and pressed his palms against the window. Outside he could see other children playing in the courtyard below. They were screaming and laughing, running between or climbing on colourful pipes cemented into the ground. He wanted to join them; he couldn't see the difference between himself and them, except that their hair was longer. He didn't understand why he wasn't allowed to be near them or why he was supposed to revere them.

Tierre joined him at the window and looked

down at the scene below.

"You can't watch them, Mecca," he said, pushing the point of his elbow into Mecca's ribs. There was a scuffle and then both boys fell on the floor, where they continued to wrestle until Tierre sat upon Mecca's back and pulled his arms painfully behind. The fight between them had been silent and even now, Mecca grit his teeth to stop himself from crying out.

"Let go," he hissed.

Tierre bent over to whisper in his ear, relieving the pressure on Mecca's shoulders. "Stop watching them, Mecca," he ordered. "Say you'll stop."

"Let me go," Mecca said, taking advantage of the lighter hold by attempting to buck Tierre off himself. It didn't work and he was rewarded a painful tug for his efforts. A groan escaped him.

"Say you'll stop," Tierre insisted.

"I'll stop," Mecca replied, but even as he said it he knew he wouldn't. His words appeased Tierre who released his arms and climbed off him. Mecca slowly got to his feet and massaged each of his shoulders in turn. "I won't stop," he amended. Tierre made a rude gesture at him.

"I'll tell Yanju Rivia you look out the window at them."

"Then I'll tell Yanju Rivia you wrestled me to the ground."

Tierre thrust his chin out before leaving Mecca behind in the empty room. He waited for his friend to shut the door after himself before he returned to the window. The girls had left the playground and were clustered around an open archway, all trying to get through at once. A girl turned to talk to one of her friends beside her when she looked upwards. Mecca didn't think she could see him until she began to wave, causing some of the girls to turn and look.

He gasped and quickly stepped backward, out of sight. His heart raced at the possibility of being spotted. He waited until he felt calmer and worked up his courage to have another look.

The courtyard below was empty and the archway that led into the building beyond was clear. All of the girls had gone inside.

Disappointed, he left the window and headed for the door. He watched it open as he approached and expected to see Tierre hurrying him up but instead it was Yanju Rivia. Mecca stopped walking, stunned that his friend truly had betrayed his location.

"Mecca?" the old man asked as if he hadn't expected to find anyone inside. "What are you doing in here?"

His Yanju looked surprised instead of angry and Mecca was unsure that Tierre had told on him after all. It could also be a ruse as Rivia could be wily.

"I come here to be alone, Yanju," Mecca replied, keeping his answer as honest as possible.

"Your clothes are filthy," Rivia replied, sounding suspicious.

"I lay down on the floor. It must be dirty."

Rivia studied Mecca long enough for his heart to pound in his chest some more but the old man was appeased.

"Go," he said, holding the door open for Mecca to scamper out. "Change your clothes," Mecca was told at his back. He hurried to the room he shared with Tierre, to do just that.

She frowned at him and shifted on the mattress, mirroring his pose so that they were both propped up on their elbow and facing each other.

"You weren't allowed to play with the girls?" she asked. He shook his head and waited for her to decide what she wanted next. The sheet had fallen to her waist, revealing two small, pert breasts. He fought the instinct to reach out and cup one of them, even though they'd recently been intimate.

"Did you have your own playtime?" she asked. He paused then shook his head. "Not ever?" she asked.

He told her about the time he began a game.

He was running around the field in a circle with nineteen other boys. The routine was so well-ingrained that Yansho Balta had left them to it, sneaking off to do whatever it was he did while the boys were supposed to be supervised. Mecca was bored with running in a circle, he wanted to have fun.

He nudged Tierre who was in step beside him and his friend looked at him inquisitively.

"Chase me," Mecca said, then sprinted away, pushing past other boys in front of him, earning some protesting cries. He chanced a look over his shoulder and his heart leaped in his mouth to see Tierre had almost gained on him and was reaching out with a big grin. Laughing, Mecca put on more speed and knocked over someone in his haste to run past them. It wasn't long before three boys were sprinting after him. Soon there was a mess of chases and a great deal of tackling. Mecca had hit the ground hard a number of times as Tierre or other boys dove for his feet. Grass stained his skin and clothes and a few bruises were gained as play turned rough.

A loud horn sounded that had all boys scrambling to line up at attention. Mecca got up more slowly and joined in the impromptu assembly. He could feel the stare of boys on him when he walked past them to fall into their ranks and also the stare of Yanju Rivia who was still holding the horn in one hand, now silent.

"You are not permitted to fight!" Yanju Rivia shouted at them, spittle flying from his lips.

"We weren't fighting," Mecca spoke up. There was a ripple of whispered conversation. "We were playing a game."

The Yanju approached Mecca, so that he could scream directly into his face. "You are not permitted to play violent games!"

Rivia was a giant to him, Mecca merely a ten year old boy, worth nothing in a civilisation that demanded obedience. His heart was racing, his head was pounding and his mouth was dry. He knew he would be punished for inspiring a game. He knew the rest of the boys would be punished for joining in. They would make sure he took another beating for it later—that was how it worked.

"We are not permitted to have fun," he argued, his voice shaking but strong. The Yansho struck him across the face with the back of his hand and Mecca fell to the ground. He slowly got to his feet and stood up, feeling blood trickling out of his nose.

He earned himself five strokes of the cane across his back for his insolence and a further three for starting the game. When he was released back into the room he shared with Tierre, his friend washed his wounds and asked him how he felt. Mecca replied that he felt it was worth it.

She didn't look horrified like he expected, but thoughtful. He hadn't anticipated this reaction from her. Tourists were shocked when he spoke of his childhood — unless this wasn't her first time visiting this world. Her lack of a reaction caused his heartbeat to accelerate with the fear she might be an auditor. If she reported that he was telling stories of rebellion and hardship to tourists…

"Do you think my life is easy, compared to yours?" she asked.

"Mistress, I am certain you are the best judge of — "

She threw herself backward upon the bed, interrupting his response. She stared at the ceiling and made no move to cover herself up. She didn't seem to want anything so he watched her until she spoke again.

"Who was your first mistress?" she asked.

He was a slave assigned to tourists so he had no mistress, but all women were his mistresses so he told her about Lillia, even though Anika was stronger in his memory.

Lessons were long and boring. He liked learning the cadence of the Authoritan language and excelled at it but everything else disinterested him. History, geography, mathematics and exercising were all stifled by routine.

Their schedule in Obedience began the usual

way but Yanju Pato had something new and exciting to offer them. They would demonstrate all they'd learned. There were looks exchanged from some of the boys to others as they guessed what a demonstration might entail but nobody dared speak.

Mecca was sitting at the long glass table in the middle of the front row, with Tierre on his right, so he was closest to the girl when she walked in with her Yanjan—a severe looking woman dressed in a gown of shimmering colours. The girl wore a simple white dress and looked nervous as she stood at the front of the room, facing twenty seated boys.

Yanju Pato addressed them.

"Student Lillia is here to test your obedience."

Mecca expected more to be said so was surprised when Pato nodded to the Yanjan and left the room. Twenty boys stared at the girl and she looked over at the woman in charge of her, who remained to one side of the room. Mecca risked a look and caught the nod that Lillia received.

"Stand up," Lillia said softly.

Mecca stood along with the rest of the boys on his row, hearing chairs being scraped backward as they followed the instruction.

"Louder," said the Yanjan.

"Stand up," Lillia repeated firmly. Nobody moved; they were all standing. "I mean, sit down."

They all sat. Lillia was encouraged by this and Mecca understood that the 'test' had a two-fold effect. They were demonstrating how obedient they could be and Lillia was experiencing what it was like to have control. It was their social grooming.

"Applaud," she said, then giggled as she received their applause. After a couple more innocuous commands, Lillia's experience ended and she was instructed by her Yanjan to leave the room. Mecca heard the praise she received and was aware of the absence of acknowledgement for them.

Another girl was shown in.

There was a lot of sitting and standing until the ninth girl, who stared at them all from the front of the room, saying nothing. Her name was Anika and she was urged to give a command but she continued to say nothing, glaring at them all instead. He shifted in his seat. The small movement was enough to attract Anika's attention. She pointed an accusatory finger at Mecca.

"You. Stand up on the table."

Mecca used his chair to step onto the table as Anika wanted.

"Take off your dress." Anika's second command was outrageous. He didn't want to be naked in front of everybody, least of all a girl and her Yanjan. His delay attracted another order barked at him.

"Take it off, now!"

There would be no help from anyone. His Yanju had left the room and the Yanjan wasn't interfering with her student's command. Mecca had been isolated because he'd caught her eye and for whatever reason, she was taking her ire out on him. If he didn't follow her instruction, he would fail his obedience test and it was impossible to determine what kind of punishment it would attract. There was no doubt it would be worse than being naked in front of his peers and this angry girl.

Mecca reached down and grabbed the hem of his skirt, pulling the clothing up over his head. He held the material in front of himself, feeling vulnerable and hiding what he could. He knew what her next order would be even before she said it.

"Drop it and you can't cover yourself up."

He looked at her before he followed her command, seeing the excited, malicious glee on her face. Her anger had turned into something else and he wanted to be out from her appraising eyes. She was looking him over. When she took a few steps towards him, Mecca's heart felt like it had leapt from his chest into his throat.

"Enough."

Anika and Mecca both looked at the Yanjan, who shook her head and beckoned Anika over and then helped her out of the room with a push. Mecca started to climb down but was stopped.

"Have you been permitted to step down?" the Yanjan asked him.

"No, but—"

"Stay up there until you are allowed to leave," she said, thankfully not berating him for his attempt at an explanation.

The next girl that entered looked surprised and embarrassed at the sight of Mecca standing naked on the table and ordered him to get down and get dressed. He wanted to thank her but wasn't sure if he was allowed so he said nothing. The rest of the girls turned out much like the first, with simple commands for all of them.

Mecca returned to the empty room during his free time but he didn't go to the window. He sat in the corner instead and huddled into a little ball, doing his best to work through his humiliation.

Later that night Tierre left his bed and crawled into Mecca's, to cuddle him.

"I don't like girls," he whispered into Mecca's ear. "They have ugly hearts."

"Only one of them had an ugly heart," Mecca replied.

"I should have said something," Tierre wished uselessly.

"There was no point. She would just make you stand beside me."

"Then I should have said something," Tierre said again and Mecca understood his friend's compassion. He was glad that Tierre had kept his silence though, because out of the two of them, he thought he was stronger.

She'd covered her breasts up when he spoke about being forced to take off his clothes. He was sure it was a gesture of compassion or unease. For either reason he was pleased she did it. He'd felt vulnerable re-telling the story and it surprised him. Many years had passed and much worse had happened in between then and now. He supposed he'd survived by focussing on the good in his life instead of the bad, unable to change it or move on.

"What happened to Tierre?"

He hesitated and she read the gloom in his eyes.

"He stood up for you one day," she guessed. But she was wrong.

In the middle of his teenage years and exploring his

sexuality with multiple partners, Mecca was superficially content with his role. He'd been chosen by Theora this afternoon and found she enjoyed being teased. Halfway through their time together she'd praised him, telling him he had the patience to suit her needs. Mecca hadn't considered it to be a matter of patience so much as light hearted fun. He supposed some of the other young men he knew would take the wrong attitude about the power she assigned them — control in sex was a delicate balance, he'd found.

He was doing his best to please her so she would select him again when a cry from another room jarred him from his mood. It had the effect of ice water, dousing his spirit and leaving him cold. He wasn't supposed to leave the room before he was permitted and certainly not before his mistress, but the rules didn't matter when it was Tierre's voice he'd heard. The shout had been made in anger, something he'd never heard from his friend before. He didn't even bother putting on his tunic and skirt before hurrying out.

The footpath was hot on his bare feet as he ran along it past small single-roomed dwellings. The sunlight was sharp in his eyes reflecting off silver dome roofs, making it difficult for him to see where he was going. He knew the sound had come from this direction and so he ran. Some doors opened and women watched him run past them, naked. He no longer cared.

He saw Tierre lying on his back in the open doorway of a dwelling. Red blossomed at the collar of his tunic. His hand was upon the wound in his throat but with no great strength. Mecca made an anguished noise that was somewhere between pain and protest before he dropped to his knees at Tierre's side.

"Tierre, please don't," he begged, unable to speak of death when it was already upon him. He didn't know what to do other than to cradle his friend's head and plead for life to return. He looked inside the room that Tierre had tried to escape and saw Anika standing in the middle of it. She was still clutching the base of the broken lamp she'd used to murder Mecca's friend with. She watched the pair of them dispassionately and Mecca despised her. He saw how her fingers tightened around the makeshift weapon when their eyes met. No doubt she could read the threat in his gaze.

He had no time to act, no time to speak. Yanju Rivia was already upon them, with Yanjans shouting orders at the girls. Anika went away with one of them, Mecca with Yanju Rivia and Tierre's body was picked up and removed by two other Yanju who Mecca didn't bother to identify.

He was punished for leaving Theora unattended but not severely so. One strike upon his back that Mecca barely felt in his grief. He asked after Anika, guessing that she would no longer be assigned a slave—a wise punishment for a mistress capable of murder, he thought. His assumption was wrong; she would still be someone's mistress. This minor transgression would be a setback to her graduation but would not impair her later.

"Killing a slave is a minor transgression?" Mecca asked, outraged. "If she selects me as bed partner I will—"

He was struck across the face hard enough to

rock back, but there was enough furniture in the way that he remained on his feet. He felt betrayed by the thunderous look on Yanju Rivia's face, who pointed a finger towards him.

"You will not finish that sentence and you will not carry out the intention," the Yanju growled at him. Mecca wanted to punch back, to strike out against him. His fists were curled but he couldn't do it. His heart was broken but his head was not. A threat against a mistress would not end well for him. Rivia was saving him.

Her eyes were wide and her mouth was closed. Mecca couldn't bear to tell her the rest; that he had been spared Anika for a year, which must have been his Yanju's doing, but then she finally selected him and he'd done his duty. It had been difficult but bearable because she hadn't taunted him with Tierre's death. He didn't tell her about Anika because if he could be intimate with the woman who'd murdered his friend then his intimacy meant nothing. So far he'd found very few women who assigned emotional importance to sex.

"I'm sorry," she said to him when she left. The apology surprised him; she had to know it was discouraged for a mistress to apologise to her slave. He thought her apology was because of Tierre's death but reconsidered. She was sorry for Mecca, not for a slave she didn't know. Tierre was a statistic, Mecca a tragedy.

He pressed his lips firmly together and watched the door close behind her. She might look at him as an object of pity because he was a slave, but telling the truth had been freeing.

PURE

He had focal enhancements implanted in his eyelids. As he closed his eyes they glowed iridescent orange. When he blinked he flashed an orange beacon like roadwork hazard lights. She was distracted by his eyes enough to over-fill his cup while pouring. The flood of aromatic coffee across the table caused the seated couple to leap up.

Frowns and angry voices turned her way before they faded awkwardly into frustration. He ended up apologising as his girlfriend gave her looks of pity. They were probably trying to be compassionate.

Be angry at me, she wanted to scream. There was nothing she could say. They'd already decided she was incapable of handling their rage. She shut off the touch-top table and used the spill-rag tucked into her apron to wipe up the mess. She cleaned up beneath a glow of orange and spared a glance to confirm that he couldn't even look at her. Irritated, she flicked the touch-top on again and walked away, leaving them to their apps and whispered conversation.

Walking home was worse than usual.

Her scarf was stolen from her bag at work. She knew who'd taken it because the other waitresses were sniggering between themselves, but she had no proof. Her boss was already uneasy about her so she didn't want to offer him a reason to dismiss her.

People saw her clearly now she had no scarf to hide beneath. Some gave her curious stares while others were openly horrified. She wanted to pull them aside and argue she was the same but it was pointless. They didn't want to understand, they were happiest judging her from a distance. She knew this from experience. A handful spared her the briefest of glances or none at all, too absorbed in their own lives to care about her. She loved those people with all her heart. They were a relief.

"Mummy, look at that lady!" A very small boy pointed her out. His mother had been ignoring her until her son made it impossible. She didn't miss the look of confused disgust and the instinctive drawing closer of the child. They were waiting at the crossing adjacent to hers and when the pedestrian light changed to green, she left them behind.

She passed a bot-kin coming the other way and they exchanged stares. These modified robotic citizens were common enough now that passing one in the street was no longer a surprise. There was a political dilemma rippling through the government about them, reported by the news apps. The government was slow to assign rights for them; they weren't entirely robotic but it was difficult to classify them as people when they'd died and been reanimated. There was lingering debate about how much human was left inside them, but now, thirty years after the first reanimation, they were mostly accepted by the public. Bot-kins committed no crimes or changed in appearance. They were constant and predictable. There was no more fear of them, no more hatred. The public had forgotten their worries... a whole generation had grown up with them after all. In spite of their placid nature, she associated more closely with Mr Orange Eyes than with the reanimated bio-tech corpses. She was horrified that they were accepted into the community but any warnings she gave were met with accusations of ignorance and hate-mongering.

Someone spat on her. She stopped with a gasp and looked at the globule of saliva sliding down her chest. It had landed on her clothes and she didn't want to wipe it away with a bare hand. She found a crumpled paper napkin in the bottom of her bag and used it to wipe the spit away. She hadn't bothered to look around at who her aggressor was. Nothing could be done about it so why give herself the added tension of looking for hostile faces in crowds?

The rest of her walk home was uneventful. She thumbed the apartment building's security pad and tapped the metal strip of her key card to the door's panel. The lock clicked open and she went inside. Living in a poorer neighbourhood meant there were no retinal scanners or weapons detection doorframes. The elevator worked but was slow. She habitually used the stairs to get to her place on the first floor.

She checked her mail and found a post-drive sent from Claire, her sister. She turned the small blue rectangle in her hands, wondering what she'd find on it. The elevator doors opened with a wheezy shudder and she began climbing stairs as two adolescent boys stepped out. She expected jeers at her retreating form but they were too absorbed in their deck of holo-cards to notice her.

After entering her apartment she took the time to properly secure the door. Her bag hung on a hook and the post-drive plugged into the television. She moved into the kitchen to make herself a tea while her sister's post-drive loaded and heard Claire's greeting as the kettle boiled. She poured hot water into her cup and listened to news about how the twins were doing. She dunked the tea-bag as Claire discussed the latest news for how to raise genius babies.

Everyone seems to be having genius babies these days, she thought, but her nieces really were likely to be brilliant. Claire was clever and her husband Royale was intensely intelligent. Bio-tech was a good field for him and he'd won many prestigious awards for his work.

As she walked into the living room carrying her cup of tea, Claire looked seriously at her from the television screen.

"Royale and I have decided to get the Ambrose enhancements, for bot-kin status."

Her legs no longer had the strength to

support her. She dropped to her knees with a clunk that she barely heard and didn't feel. Her hands fell loose at her sides and tea seeped into the rug beside a shattered cup.

"No," she moaned, but it was an unheard protest. Her sister Claire had likely sent her this news via a recording for a reason, instead of calling her up and chatting in real time.

"I know how you feel about them, but—"

No, you don't know how I feel about them, she thought among an emotional tide of anger, misery and helplessness while her sister went on to explain the new research Royale had uncovered and the new laws which had recently passed. *You don't understand why I live like I do, so how can you know how I feel?*

It was obvious Claire sent a recording because she hadn't wanted a discussion on the matter. There was no desire to explain to her crazy sister about rational things like turning herself into a bot-kin. Enhancements were the way of the future, so why not upload your personality into a computer chip, inject it into your brain and replace your body from the neck down with the latest robotic machination?

She heard the rest even though she didn't want to. Claire was undergoing the procedure before Royale because her paperwork had returned first. She was doing it on the morning of the twentieth. Yesterday morning. The process would be complete on the night of the twenty-second. Tomorrow evening.

Claire would no longer age and she would forever be immune to diseases. Claire would raise her daughters without fear of an early death. She would always be around for them. It had nothing to do with the fact Royale was dying of cancer. It had nothing to do with watching each of their parents wasting away of terminal illnesses while they were young girls. Royale had intended to go through the procedure himself and Claire was convinced that it suited her as well.

Her thoughts went to her six month old nieces. The latest legislation had been passed; the passive nature of the bot-kins had proven they were not unsafe parents. They were patient, reasonable and logical. Emotions didn't impair their judgment. They could access the public mainframe and forever have all the answers downloaded to their consciousness. They were considered highly evolved; they were pure.

She was a social monstrosity; a joke, a zealot, a non-conformist. She was spat on in the street and looked upon with pity because of her obvious display of extremist thinking. She was not tattooed, she had no piercings, and she had no enhancements. She didn't even use cosmetics.

How abnormal she was, for not wishing to medicate or suppress her negative emotions.

How ignorant she was, for refusing to enhance her intelligence.

How arrogant she was, to embrace her flaws and force others to as well.

How helpless she was, to watch the world spin into madness around her while wondering if she was the crazy one after all.

MIRROR

It was getting dark and Imogen wanted to stop for the night. The same conversation rolled around when she told Nick they should've made a reservation and he replied there would be vacancies everywhere. Imogen tried not to repeat herself again though she continued to worry about being stranded, because of the kids.

Behind her she could hear Lucy reading licence plates of each passing car, making up words with the trio of letters. When they'd left for home this morning it had been cute, even funny. Now it grated on her nerves and she wished guiltily that Lucy would shut up and fall asleep like her brother David in the baby seat beside her.

"Pea, kay, tea. Packet!" Lucy declared with four year old authority as a sedan bearing that licence combination passed them. Her attention moved onto the next car. "Bee, bee, el. Bubble!"

"What's the name of the next town, again?" Imogen asked, trying to put Lucy's piping voice at the back of her mind. She knew she'd already been told but she was tired and it was hard to think.

"Grant Creek," Nick replied, pulling into the turnoff lane. "We'll stay there the night."

"Thank God," Imogen muttered and Nick smiled at her, his hazel eyes sparkling in the fading light. She knew he found her impatience amusing. She wondered how almost nothing could rattle him. It was a skill she'd tried to master as long as she could remember. Whenever he told her not to worry it was like she'd lost yet another battle. She was anxious about everything; the kids, their careers, not having a reservation.

"Eff, you, sea—"

"Lucy!" she said crossly, then realised her daughter hadn't yet said anything to go with those letters. "Um, do you want a chocolate?" Nick snorted laughter and she gave him a warning look which he conveniently missed.

"Chocolate?" Lucy repeated, her interest piqued. She'd forgotten about the letters but when Imogen checked the glove box there were only empty wrappers. She shouldn't have interrupted the natural progression. What did it matter if Lucy said the swearword? It wasn't like she'd never said it before. It had been harrowing the first time around though, and Imogen didn't want Lucy to regain her fascination with them. She'd been embarrassed enough when Lucy had said every swear word she'd learned for two weeks. It had been enough time for Imogen to grow weary of the disapproving stares from other mothers.

"You can have one after dinner," she promised, hoping Lucy would be content with this. Lucy cheered softly, wary that her treat might be taken away if she woke up David beside her.

"Did you see that sign back there?" Nick asked with a broad grin. "It said 'Welcome to Grant Creek, Queensland. Pop two thousand something."

"Pop," Lucy said in the back seat with a giggle.

"Pop is short for population," Imogen explained. She wondered if Lucy would continue questioning but didn't.

"Would a town that small have a motel?"

"Every town has a motel," Nick said in a reassuring tone. "I'll bet it's above the public bar."

"That's a hotel, not a motel," she corrected him, wondering if she wanted to walk the kids past a bunch of drunks.

"Whatever."

Two high pitched beeps sounded out of Imogen's handbag at her feet and she removed her phone from it.

"There's no service," she said worriedly. She looked out the windscreen at the road as it headed deeper into the bush. "The GPS won't work."

"It's okay, honey. GPS will still work even without a signal. It's not like we're in the middle of the bush, either."

The calm tone that had calmed her nerves before now made her feel like she was being patronised. She was about to snap a reply when the first few buildings began to show. They'd arrived in town but when Imogen checked her phone, there was still no service.

Nick drove down the main street, which had no other traffic on it.

"There aren't any people around," he said.

She wasn't too surprised, as a township like Grant Creek likely couldn't offer much by way of attractions.

"Maybe they're at home watching television," Imogen said wryly.

"Maybe 'Peppa Pig' is on!" Lucy suggested.

Nick laughed and nodded. "Maybe it is, Lu."

They drove on in silence for a few minutes.

"Huh," Nick grunted and pulled over. Imogen didn't know what he was looking at. She couldn't see anything particularly odd. There were a few more houses, some trees and the road ahead.

"What is it, Daddy?"

"It's the end of the town." Nick turned to Imogen apologetically and she understood what he wasn't saying.

"There's no hotel, is there." She meant it as a question but it came out as a statement.

"Do we have to sleep in the car?" Lucy asked, excited at the prospect of camping in the car overnight. Imogen couldn't match Lucy's enthusiasm.

"We might've passed it," she suggested with a positivity she didn't feel.

"Let's turn around and check again," he said and reached over to touch her knee before performing a U-turn that took up the whole road. "Where is everybody?"

"It's after six, they're all inside their homes because it's getting dark."

Nick glanced at her but said nothing.

Lucy yelled out behind them, causing David to grumble and stir in his seat. "There's a man! Look!" She pointed ahead of them, her finger accusatory but helpful. "He can tell us where the hotel is!"

"Lu, use your quiet voice," Nick said. Lucy immediately hushed, likely she was still anticipating the chocolate she had been promised.

Imogen looked at the man as Nick drove toward him. He was standing underneath a bright yellow awning, the type Imogen had seen only in Hollywood movies depicting 'quaint little towns'. He was bent slightly forward, leaning on a cane. He wore a dark shirt and long pants, clothes that she didn't expect to be worn in this hot climate. Then Nick moved the car to the side of the road and pulled up beside him. Imogen saw this man was leaning on a cane.

She rolled down the window as the man watched from his position on the footpath. She wondered why he wasn't coming up to the car. Surely he could see that they wanted to talk to him?

"Excuse me," she began and waited for the man to acknowledge her presence before continuing. He cocked his head as if puzzled that she was addressing him. Undaunted, she went on. "Could you tell me where the hotel is around here?"

The man remained silent.

Nick leaned over in his seat and spoke to the man himself.

"Is there a hotel in this town?"

The man shook his head. He shuffled closer to the car but stopped within a metre of it. Then he smiled and Imogen was amazed by the number of wrinkles that lined his face. At her first guess she would've put him at eighty but now it looked as though he was at the century.

"You can go on to the next town," the man said in a voice that was surprisingly deep and robust. "That'd be Shepherd's Knot, but they got their farm show on so I don't like your chances."

Nick settled back into his own seat and Imogen threw him her 'I told you so' look because she didn't want to say it. The man approached the car and bent down so he could look through the window. Imogen felt uncomfortable being so close to him, uncertain as to why. There was nothing distasteful about him.

"I got a phone in the shop if you want to call around," he offered with a smile.

"Thank you," Imogen said and as Nick switched off the engine she opened the car door, careful to give the old man time to move away. She watched as Nick rescued David from the baby seat, the eighteen month old awakening from his nap. Imogen unplugged Lucy from her booster seat and had to stand back as Lucy hopped out herself and close the car door on her own. She didn't like things done for her.

"The phone's on the counter at the back of the shop." The man grinned at Imogen and gave her a sly wink. "You can let your kids run wild Mrs, they won't break anything."

Imogen didn't like the implication that her kids were the type to 'run wild' but she smiled politely as Nick replied for her.

"I seriously doubt that.' He gave Lucy a warning look and settled David more comfortably on his left side.

"I won't break anything."

"I bet."

"Daddy—" Lucy said painfully. Nick smiled at her to let her know he was only joking but Imogen could see that their daughter was still upset.

"The name's Joe," the man said as he turned to enter the store. Despite his presence of the cane and the shuffling movements he'd made earlier, Joe strode into his shop. He had a slight limp on his left but it was hardly noticeable. Imogen wondered if his previous motions had been ingenuine and why he would fake something like that.

"Wow," Nick breathed upon entering the shop. Imogen followed closely behind with Lucy's hand in hers. When she saw what was inside the small shop, she paused in awe at her surroundings. Lucy took her chance and pulled away, immediately losing herself in the aisles.

It was a curio shop. She couldn't remember the last time she'd seen anything that even resembled what she was seeing now. The closest she'd ever come to being in a place like this was after her eighteenth birthday when her mother had dragged her to a house where a woman gave palm readings. The house that the woman lived in had been filled to the ceiling with strange items; from potions to voodoo dolls and from tarot cards to crystal balls, but compared to this shop, that collection would have died in shame.

From where she was standing directly in front of the door, she could see nearly everything within the shop. On her left were sculptures of dragons, wizards and castles with spiralling towers. Beside those were articles of furniture; chairs and tables with gremlins carved into the legs, or rocking chairs with snake carvings. Out of the corner of her eye she could see suits of armour and ancient weapons beside them. The collection wasn't only extensive, it actually looked complete.

Twice, as she investigated the aisles, an item caught her eye and she reached for it. Both times she stopped, not knowing what it was that held her back from picking it up. She likened it to a magnet; as though it promised to make a connection with her but they ended up polar opposites instead and she was repelled at the last minute.

"Jen?" Nick's voice woke her from her reverie. "Are you coming?"

"Let her look, let her look," Joe's voice drifted from the back of the shop. "These things should not be rushed."

"Coming," Imogen called and hurried over in the direction of where the voices had come from. She couldn't see them and yet the shop was so tiny. Like an overflowing cupboard.

She walked carefully down the centre aisle, feeling displaced. The strange sensation had begun to fall on her as soon as she entered the shop and as she walked further, she felt more and more like she'd travelled back in time or to some parallel world where she was living a completely different life—as though she'd pursued a different career path, met a different man, had different children with him. She'd forgotten why she wanted to go to the back of the shop but knew she had to get there.

A man in his thirties stepped into view at the end of the aisle. He was attractive, with brown hair and hazel eyes. He held a chubby little boy in his arms and it was from looking at David that Imogen was jolted back into the present. She looked back at Nick and decided not to mention that she hadn't recognised him for a moment.

"You must've had a good look around," Nick told her.

"A couple of minutes isn't much time for a good look," Imogen replied, wondering why he was rushing her. He still had to call the hotel.

"You took more than a couple of minutes, Jen. I booked a room at Shepherd's Knob and got caught up talking with Joe. I thought you'd be pissed at me for taking so long."

"Language," Imogen said habitually as she turned to look out the window, but the shop's items covered her view. She looked at her phone instead and was stunned to see it was half past six. Where had thirty minutes gone?

"I've booked us a room, it turns out that—"

A shriek caused Imogen's heart to leap as she recognised her daughter's cry.

"Lu?" she called out worriedly, hurrying along the ends of the aisles and looking up each one. "Lucy?"

"I found something!" Lucy said, her delight now apparent in her voice and Imogen could feel herself relaxing a little, though she didn't give up on her frantic search. She'd had the strange idea that something in the shop had hurt Lucy on purpose. She found Lucy halfway up an aisle kneeling in front of a mirror. She was running a hand lovingly over the sculptured gold frame.

"Isn't it pretty?" she asked. "Can I have it for

my room?"

"It might be too expensive," Imogen said, joining Lucy in front of the mirror. Their reflections looked back wonderingly, capturing all of the light in the room and reflecting it back in a way that gave it depth.

"How much is it?" she heard Nick asking. Imogen quickly glanced around the frame but there was no obvious price tag. Joe didn't appear to need one.

"The flawed diamond mirror, eh?" he said. Imogen was puzzled that a rectangular mirror would be named such a thing. "That one's a hundred and fifty."

It was a fantastic price, for the quality. Everyone was silent and Imogen felt the anticipation mount until she couldn't hold back any further.

"We'll take it!"

She tore her eyes away from her reflection to see Nick gaping at her. She wasn't usually the spontaneous one, the spend-thrift, the compulsive buyer. She'd never found anything she wanted more than this mirror, though.

"Looks like both ladies have luxurious tastes," Joe said with a chuckle. He began to move past Nick but as soon as he got within sight of David—still in Nick's arms—their son began to scream and fight.

"What the hell?" Nick asked, struggling to hold onto him. "Davy, stop it!"

Joe quickly backed away and David's tantrum instantly ended, the only evidence it had even happened where the streaks of tears down his cheeks.

"Do you take credit cards?" Imogen asked, sure that Joe would at least have a machine for EFTPOS. She was shocked when he shook his head.

"I'm afraid it's cash only."

Imogen was astounded. Who operated on a cash-only basis nowadays? She only had a fifty dollar note in her purse and doubted he would let her have the mirror for so great a discount. Nick set David down and pulled out his wallet. He pulled out a fifty and a twenty then shrugged at her.

"Would you let us have it for a hundred and twenty?" she asked, giving her best smile to Joe and hearing the hopefulness in her own voice.

"I can do that, Mrs. I see it's all you have," Joe agreed.

Imogen handed her money to Nick who in turn handed it to Joe. She picked up David who'd moved over to cling to her legs, surprised that he hadn't poked, pulled or tasted every item on the shelves.

"I'll get the kids sorted," she said.

Lucy hopped into her booster seat on her own and David was surprisingly placid when she clicked him into place.

"Can I have my chocolate now?" Lucy asked as she was harnessed into place.

"At the hotel," Imogen said and was relieved when Nick exited the store carrying the mirror. He popped the boot open and Imogen watched him lay it across their suitcases.

"Do I have your approval?" he asked her. Imogen wasn't sure whether Nick was in a good mood or not. He was smiling but sometimes that didn't mean he was pleased. Perhaps he was annoyed at spending so much money on the mirror. If this was the case, damn him. He was the reason for their money problems, not her.

"Yes," she said, in case his question was innocent. They both got into the car and left Grant Creek behind.

Their room at the hotel was surprisingly spacious and the kids were exploring every bit of it. They seemed glad to get out of the cramped confinement of the car. Nick was lying on the bed scrolling through news apps on his phone and Imogen had pulled out her book to finish reading. She couldn't concentrate, she was stealing glances at the partly shut bathroom door. The mirror was in there because she hadn't wanted to leave it in the boot of their car. She'd insisted it come up to the room with them and Nick had complied without comment. For some reason unbeknownst to her, the intense desire to have it near her was now foreshadowed by a growing concern that it wasn't a natural, normal piece of glass.

She'd asked Nick to put it back in the car but he'd protested that she was being unreasonable. After some arguing that had started out softly for the kids' sake, Nick moved the mirror into the bathroom. He'd had to do it himself because she was worried that she would fall under its hypnotic spell again.

A delighted squeal sounded from the bathroom; the same sound Lucy made when she'd discovered the damned thing in the first place.

Nick and Imogen both moved at the same time to investigate, when David came barrelling out of the bathroom. He slammed into Nick and attached himself to his father's legs, screaming. Imogen was spooked by the contrast—why was David so terrified when Lucy sounded so gleeful?

Imogen took a few more steps to the bathroom door but Lucy made an appearance, holding something in her cupped hands.

Her mind jumped on a few different ideas what it was Lucy held. At first it looked like a lightbulb that was somehow lit up by itself. Then it looked like a piece of coloured crystal. When Lucy's fingers moved around it, Imogen was startled by her impression of a giant eyeball.

"I found a diamond," Lucy said enthusiastically. When she held it up, Imogen's mind made the final connection and she could understand what she was looking at.

"Where did you get that?" Nick asked, prying a sobbing David off his leg. He shifted the boy to one side and ignored his cries in order to inspect the gem in Lucy's hands. Imogen reached out to comfort him but David headed for the safety of the bed instead, crawling beneath it.

"It has a light blue flaw in the centre," Nick said to Imogen, who was caught between going to her frightened toddler or inspecting the thing Lucy had found. She knew David was safe where he was, that he felt secure so she moved to her husband and daughter. She looked at the diamond in Nick's hands and saw the peculiar blue sphere in the middle. She reached out to touch it but Nick moved it away from her outstretched hand. He ignored the sharp look she gave him.

"Where did you find this?" he demanded. Imogen recognised the glimmer in his hazel eyes and the anxious tone of his voice—it was excitement. Pure, greedy excitement. She'd seen it on his face when he'd won big at the casino last year. She'd heard it in his voice when he'd told her he could win it all back after losing it all. It was never enough. There had to be more. This trip was supposed to remind him that his family was more valuable than some plastic chips. It was supposed to show him what money could buy, instead of a dealt hand or a spinning wheel of red and black.

"In the mirror."

Imogen didn't doubt her daughter's words but had trouble comprehending them. How could something like a diamond come out of a flat surface like a mirror? But she knew. Even as she made herself ask the logical questions in her head, she knew. It was the reason Nick had called the sphere in the centre of the diamond a 'flaw' instead of something more descriptive. He'd used that word because Joe had used that word.

The flawed diamond mirror.

"Come look!" Lucy ran back into the bathroom and Nick followed. Imogen hurried in after them, unable to talk because all of the spit in her mouth had disappeared. The light was too bright in here; it made her feel tingly and surreal. There was only one thing on her mind; keep her daughter away from the mirror. She had to grab Lucy and run.

She froze instead when she realised the light source was coming from the mirror itself. Nick knelt down in front of the mirror and set the diamond down on the floor. With both hands he gripped the mirror and spun it around to look at the back.

"What are you doing, Daddy? Why is he doing that, Mummy?" Lucy asked, swapping her questions from Nick to Imogen. She eventually grew silent when not given an answer. Imogen knew what he was looking for; he was looking for the trick. He was trying to figure out how the mirror was projecting light. Imogen could see a small line of black writing in the corner.

"This makes no sense," Nick said.

"What does it say?" Imogen wasn't sure if he was talking about the writing or the fact the mirror seemed to be glowing all by itself.

"Two flaws must be replaced by one."

"Is it a riddle?" Lucy asked.

"Yes, honey." Imogen was certain the line was a riddle. Or a warning. "Let's just leave it alone, Nick."

Nick ignored her and turned the mirror back around. The bathroom was washed with the ethereal light of the mirror once again.

"How did you get the diamond, Lu?" Nick asked. When the answer didn't come fast enough he shouted at her. "Lu, pay attention! How did you get the diamond?" he pointed at the large gem on the floor.

"It's in the mirror, inside. I could see it so I reached in and took it."

The explanation was simple and horrific. Imogen shook her head but Nick was intent on seeing the results for himself.

"Don't!" Imogen screamed and yanked Lucy close to her. Normally Lucy would object or cry but she was silent as they both watched Nick reach his arm all the way in to his elbow. It was like looking at an illusionist performing a very smooth trick but she knew there was no trick here. Just magic. When Nick reached in further, all the way to his shoulder, Imogen couldn't keep her silence. "Nick, for fuck's sake!"

"I have another one!" Nick shouted. Imogen wanted to join David underneath the bed. If this was what he'd seen Lucy do, then she could understand his terror. She remained where she was, knowing that if she stepped out of the bathroom now, she would take the kids and go.

Nick finally pulled his arm out of the mirror completely and was holding a diamond with a light blue flaw in the centre, exactly like the first one. He set it down beside the other and was about to reach in again when Lucy's scream stopped him.

"Only two, Daddy! Only two!"

Imogen was still holding onto her daughter but now she looked frantically around the bathroom.

"It's okay, honey. That means one left," he said to her in his matter-of-fact voice. Imogen made a move for the drawer, to see if there was a hairdryer inside — or something equally weighty to smash against the mirror — but Lucy gripped onto her tightly, restricting her movements.

It was too late anyway. Nick had rolled the dice again and reached into the mirror a second time. A second time for him but he'd gambled the warning meant each person, not overall. He couldn't be happy with two huge diamonds that were probably millions of dollars each. He couldn't be happy with the life he already had. He couldn't be happy with one thing when he knew there was more to be had. She'd always known that about him but tolerated it, because his greed hadn't made him selfish. He was a flawed man.

Imogen thought she understood. She managed to grab him before he was pulled into the mirror by some unseen force. She had a hold of his middle and could feel herself being dragged towards the mirror, which had widened somehow to allow entry for Nick's broad shoulders. Imogen could feel warmth radiating out from the mirror. The light was now so bright that she had to screw her eyes tightly shut. She screamed for Lucy to close her eyes, for many different reasons.

Her grip was slipping. She could feel it sliding from his waist and down to his thighs. She tried to hold on but now the heat was searing her face. Nick was kicking out with his legs which made her job a great deal more difficult. She felt small hands gripping the sides of her shirt and knew Lucy was trying to help. It was still no good. Imogen was being dragged toward the mirror herself as well as her daughter.

Her grip slipped completely and she was thrown against the tub with Lucy between her and the porcelain bath. Her daughter wailed over her smacked head. Nick's legs were disappearing into the mirror and the light had gone from red to pink. Imogen lunged for him and managed to get his ankle. He was mostly still now; one of his legs was twitching and she tried not to think about what that meant but she could feel her throat clogging with sobs.

She thought about breaking the mirror anyway but now she wasn't sure she could—whatever she smashed against it would likely travel through to the other side.

The other side, where Nick was going right now.

Whatever was pulling Nick was very strong because it was pulling her in too. She was aware she'd have to either let Nick go or be pulled inside after him, leaving her children behind. It wasn't an easy choice but she was spared from making it as her grip on Nick's feet was wrenched from her.

"No!" she yelled. Tears streamed down her eyes. She groped around in the mirror and her hand bumped against something cold and hard. She grabbed it and pulled it out.

When she looked at it, the warning made a horrific kind of sense.

Two flaws must be replaced by one.

What she was holding was a diamond.

It had a hazel flaw in the centre.

THE SONG

The river sings to me. I throw it plastic gems as gifts and when they run out, my mother's jewellery goes next. Small ferries bob along the surface and I wave. Someone always waves back. The water's edge beckons like a newly made friend, inviting me to play. Toes dressed in sandals are dipped before I am gathered inside by stern hands, lectured on the price of shoes as we return to the house.

Over my shoulder the river keens for me.

The sounds of the city grow dull as the river's melody soars. Bridges pass overhead and the rhythmic slapping of the paddlewheel keeps in time with the music. The breeze is warm and gentle, as are the hands on my waist. As he lowers to one knee and presents me with a ring, the song reaches a climactic pause. I take it and remember the offerings I made to the river as a child but this is something I keep for myself. A car horn interrupts an unfinished melody and I know I've betrayed my love. My choice is clear when I admire the ring on my finger.

Tears and shattered plates hold more meaning than our words to one another. Ceramic shards are swept into the bin. I wish I could dispose of my ill thoughts as easily. The wind funnels down the side of the house and I tighten my cardigan's embrace. I allow myself to be pushed along and look out over the river from the patio. My hair and clothes can't decide which way up to fall. Am I forgiven? As my eyelids close I hear the music. It is soothing and ethereal with a familiar ebb and flow. It warms my heart as the wind chills me. When I am gathered inside by strong hands, my palms are red and my fingers hurt to unfurl.

Over my shoulder the song fades beneath my baby's cries.

The river cuts through a garden of grey and green. Mud brown is striped white by watercraft and I linger at my apartment window as patterns cross and repeat beneath me. From this height I cannot hear the river's song but I know it is calling. With a jealous eye I watch as the rowing club fly their canoes along the water's surface. I force myself to turn my back and watch my children play. Their father has not concerned himself with them for years and we have nobody else.

Water sloshes against rocks in the wake of a hasty catamaran. Nobody waves back. I lower a wrinkled hand to steady myself, feet insecure in practical shoes. Geisha steps bring me to a place where I crouch and look into the murk. The river's song is stronger now; I can hear it but it is still muffled. Curious, I extend a foot and submerge it. Like an antenna positioned correctly, the song fills my heart with cool adulation. It is distinct and inspiring.

Now that I stand waist-deep, I understand the river has always belonged to me and me to it. There is nothing left for me on the surface. My children are no longer small and have little to say to me. I see their haunted eyes and smiles of pity for they do not understand why I hum or where the tune comes from. They think they know best.

I no longer want anything except the eternal embrace of my lifelong love. As I sink to the silted floor, I become an extra note in the river's melody.

Thank you

Thank you for reading.
Thank you for being a reader.
Thank you for buying books.
Thank you for supporting writers.
Thank you for supporting me.

MORE BOOKS
BY DELIA STRANGE

NOVELS
Femme (Light)

**WANDERER OF WORLDS BOOK SERIES
(WITH LINDA CONLON)**
Axiom
Untethered
Transition

NON-FICTION
The Streetwise Motorcyclist

If you enjoy short stories, I do my best to release a short story every month to my newsletter subscribers, though writing a multiple book series (*Wanderer of Worlds*) might lead to a few late newsletters. Subscribers also receive a free e-book as thanks. It is randomly chosen and sent to you on sign-up.
You can sign up on my website:

www.DeliaStrange.com

Cheers.

Femme (Light)
A Wanderer Novel

**Science fantasy with a touch of romance.
Utopia with a touch of slavery.**

Kaley Blackburn is sent to Femme in her final year of Future Tech studies. The world is a socialist utopia of low crime, great health and advancements in technology that leave other worlds envious.

It's a fantastic place to visit if you're a woman. Men, on the other hand, are the slaves that tend to all feminine desires. Kaley knew about the world's cultural aspect of slavery but didn't expect that she would have to participate.

Mecca is handsome, intelligent and obedient but every answer he gives to Kaley's questions only feed her growing concerns. Does Femme hide an ugly truth beneath its glamorous surface and can she trust her feelings for a man obligated to make her feel special?

Available Now

Axiom

Wanderer of Worlds: Book One

If the worlds don't kill them,
the Authorities will.

Daeson of Cloverlea has the ability to know when people are lying. He thinks his gift makes life simple except he can still be deceived.

Synjan Walker is a fixer; relied upon to solve problems in the criminal underbelly of Gredann. She is strong-minded, capable and loyal to a fault.

When Hawke Aron of Donovan Court is torn from his home, he discovers that he has Wanderer blood. By the time he learns to control his power, he is at the mercy of a ruthless enemy.

The Authorities are innovators, technological giants and world pioneers. They charge a fortune for Interworld travel via their manufactured portal. When Wanderers shift worlds, an Authority Hunter is sent to track down and exterminate them.

Available Now

www.ingramcontent.com/pod-product-compliance
Lightning Source LLC
Chambersburg PA
CBHW021021120726
47905CB00009B/3121